# Just Call Me Clint

'Just call me Clint,' he told the town the day he rode in and Wolflock would never be the same again.

To some he looked like a drifter, whilst others were sure he spelt trouble. Whatever he was, Clint was different from anyone they'd seen before. Here was a man with a past who'd come to their town to avenge a great wrong.

Clint would either succeed, or go down shooting. He was that breed of man.

*By the same author*

Hondo County Gundown
Too Many Notches
Blood Justice
The Chosen Gun

# Just Call Me Clint

Chad Hammer

**A Black Horse Western**

ROBERT HALE · LONDON

ISBN 978-0-7090-8252-1

Robert Hale Limited
Clerkenwell House
Clerkenwell Green
London EC1R 0HT

Typeset by
Derek Doyle & Associates, Shaw Heath
Printed and bound in Great Britain by
Antony Rowe Limited, Wiltshire

# CHAPTER 1

# ONE STRANGER TOO MANY

The man named Clint knelt on one knee on a grassy bank beside the river, cupped his hands into the water and drank. As he rose to his feet, some sharp-honed, outdoor sense warned him he was no longer alone.

For a moment he froze, but only for a moment.

Lazy-seeming, he turned away as though to observe the impressive flow of the heavy green waters sliding by. As he did so, his right hand closed over a Colt handle, he dropped into a crouch and whirled with the big gun in his fist, startling the stranger sitting his saddle on the fringe of the treeline less than fifty yards distant.

The man also had gun in hand but Clint's anticipation and speed caught him but half-ready, and he appeared undecided whether to lower the weapon or make a try at using it.

'Drop that piece or I'll kill you!'

Clint had a deep voice that went with his lean physique. He thumb-cocked his piece with an ominous click and extended the barrel in the horseman's direction.

'Judas Priest, all right, all right!' the stranger gasped and his weapon thudded into the grass.

'Come here!'

Clint's voice cracked. The man had almost got the jump on him, and as he drew closer he saw that he was rat-faced and vicious of eye, with scars on his face that spoke of violence. Scum!

At another time, this tall man from the north country might well have gone easy and let the would-be robber off with a warning. But this was here and now, and that was a high danger-time for any man who threatened to get between Clint Eastman and the cause that had brought him south.

'Think of this the next man you think of jumping!' he growled, and felled the hardcase with a vicious cut of a gunbarrel that felled him to ground as though shot.

For a long moment he stood staring down at the motionless figure, for the first time truly understanding the anger and lust for revenge that had brought him south.

Moments later he was in the saddle and pushing on.

He appeared out of nowhere on a clear border morning long before the sun was up, even ahead of the time when Harry Jorgenson's red rooster got to stretch its dusty wings and crow its announcement of the new day across the sleeping rooftops of Wolflock.

He came quietly through the early coolness of what

would prove to be yet another hot New Mexican day, to cross the plank bridge over the Carmel River and make his way along by the railroad tracks, heading for the main street. He was a stranger on a dusty red horse who might have made it all the way to the Border Hotel unnoticed, but for the sheriff.

Ike Watson was the first abroad today as he was most days of the week, including Sundays.

On any given morning citizens in their beds, drifting somewhere between sleep and waking, might hear the steady clomping of boots on sun-warped planking while darkness still shrouded the alleyways – the comforting sound that announced Sheriff Watson was up and about and ready to begin another of his fourteen-hour days handling a job that could easily have kept three or four lawmen busy.

Stirring sorghum into his first pannikin of powerful black coffee in the dimness of the adobe jailhouse, Watson moved to the barred front window at the sound of a soft clip-clopping in the dust, and thus was Wolflock's first citizen to clap eyes on the man later to become known only as Clint.

Suddenly the coffee tasted bitter despite his regular three heaped teaspoons of sorghum. The leisurely passing by of the straight-backed stranger on that long-legged horse left Wolflock's one-man law force shaking his head wearily and telling himself that the long day stretching ahead just seemed to have gotten a little longer.

At the receiving end of the sheriff's critical appraisal, Clint was making his own assessment of a place he'd never seen before, yet which he'd known about all his twenty-five years.

Apart from the huge and imposing block of the flourishing business district surrounding the rail depot, the buildings of New Town were spread across a sizable area of desert where they'd stood for years, naked and exposed beneath a harsh New Mexican sun.

The railroad had come through, roughly following the line of the border, four years ago now. As predicted it had brought prosperity with it but, as was mostly the case, this prosperity did not extend to the whole town but only to the selected few.

Significantly, the high iron of the South-west split the town in half. On the south side, Old Town was shaded by ancient sequoias and inhabited by old Mexican families whose ancestors had been living there for generations. On the other hand, most of New Town was just that – new. It comprised big-business buildings, hotels and saloons, assay offices, saddleries and stores, all more modern in design and materials and contrasting sharply with the untidy sprawl of a sleepy border sheeptown.

New Town was aggressively dominated by the imposing group of buildings standing right by the tracks with a handsome sign which read:

BOWDEN AND CO. FORWARDING AND
COMMISSION AGENTS.

The newcomer's weary-gaited mount swung in at the Long Rail saloon. The rider stepped down stiffly. He mounted the steps and knocked loudly.

Sudden sharp sounds carry a long distance on an undisturbed morning.

By the time a disgruntled saloonkeeper appeared at his

doors in nightshirt and stockingette cap, it seemed half the town was awake and wondering just who in hell was raising all the racket at such an hour.

While just one man, nursing a lukewarm cup of coffee at the jail and massaging his as yet unshaven jaw, was convinced he already knew the answer.

Trouble.

Ike Watson believed he had a real nose for that commodity and his generous beak had started in twitching the moment that stranger rode by.

The peace officer of Wolflock sighed. With rustlers and brawling miners he had as much trouble to handle as he reckoned he needed. Wolflock promised to get much worse before it got any better – so who needed added trouble?

The focus of the good sheriff's concern was now perched upon a high stool at the bar of the Long Rail sipping cold beer and telling the still befuddled saloon-keeper in a quiet yet commanding tone that he would have pan-fried steak with eggs sunny side up. And he would have them now.

Slim Forte swaggered into the Commission House in a store-bought crimson shirt and snug fitting dungarees. Handsome, lithe and and cocky, the youthful gambler-cum-hellraiser with the tied-down gun and the growing reputation around Chavez County winked at a pale clerk hunched over his abacus, then cast his dark gaze around the cavernous interior, looking for sign of Bowden's niece.

The heavy-set man with the spade beard leaning on the bacon and lard display case some distance away stiffened at sight of the young rider, then shot an uncertain glance in the direction of the main offices in back. This was the security boss of Bowden & Co. and his instructions regarding Mr Slim Forte were uncertain; he knew Mr Bowden didn't really want the fellow hanging about, yet he had not actually ordered him to keep him out.

Reading the man's indecision like large print, Forte threw him a cheery wave across the hardware counter.

'Relax, Kidd, you old fuss-budget. This is a social call and I'm about the most social geezer you're likely to see all this livelong day.'

The man's relief showed plain. Forte appeared to be in good humor for a change, which Jim Kidd interpreted as a good excuse not to brace him. Was he scared? A heavyweight security man was not supposed to be scared of anybody. But Jim Kidd was most definitely relieved, although this feeling was tinged with anxiety as the dark head and trim figure of the boss-man's niece appeared through warehouse aisles of shelves groaning under their laden weight of tea and green coffee. Mr Bowden certainly didn't want his niece hobnobbing with the likes of Slim Forte. But as the girl was high-spirited and the hardcase unpredictable, Kidd wisely found something else which required his urgent attention over by the corn and oats.

'Hi, beautiful!'

'Hello, Slim. What brings you to town today?'

'Maybe you ain't noticed, Rachel, but this child's in town most days of late.'

'I have noticed.' The girl half-smiled. 'So has uncle.'

'Hmm, old uncle, huh?' Forte stroked his jaw and glanced at the windows of the office which overlooked the quarter-acre of shelved, stacked, displayed, stored and simply piled-high stacks of just about every description of trade goods available in the South-west. 'And just how is

Mr Bowden's liver this fine afternoon, anyway?'

'Testy, I would say.' Rachel folded her arms. She was a trim and pretty young woman with the raven hair and olive complexion of her Mexican mother and the blue eyes and physical vigor of her father. Like her cousins, Cole and Jim, Rachel was employed at the Commission House but worked part-time while the boys were full-time employees.

There was a flourishing social life for upper-class women in Wolflock and Rachel was an active if not always enthusiastic part of this. The girl had many admirers, amongst whom Slim Forte was one. She liked him, as did many a woman, but was also wary. The man's reputation was shady and her uncle did not care for him one little bit.

She lowered her voice and added, 'You really shouldn't come here.'

His response was to lean back and drape himself lazily over a half-opened bale of ginghams and calicoes, graceful as a dancer, cartridge-belt gleaming brassily.

'It's a free country, Sugar.'

'Please, don't call me that.'

'Why? Thought you liked it.'

'Not here. Why did you come, Slim?'

He found a piece of straw protruding from a bale, plucked it clear and set it between even teeth, sober now.

'Well, seein' as you asked, Rache, what about the dance Saturday night?'

'What about it?'

'Wanna go with yours truly?'

'No, she doesn't.'

The couple turned as the brothers appeared from one of the man-made caverns formed by the goods that had been unloaded off the freight cars in back to be stacked until finding their ways to the ranches and towns on either side of the border. Dark Cole and fair-headed Jim greeted Forte stiffly but he gave no sign of acknowledgment. He was looking peeved, no novelty to those who knew him.

'Please, I can handle this,' Rachel protested.

'Not sure you can, Rachel,' said the one who had spoken. He gestured. 'If you're not buying, Slim. . . .' He left the sentence unfinished, gesturing at the doors.

'Or else?' Forte's voice was soft, dark eyebrows lifting quizzically, looking in that moment every bit as dangerous as a copperhead. 'Don't tell me Fetch and Carry are goin' to toss me out?'

That was his nickname for them. The brothers hated it. But they did not bite. Softly, softly was the sensible way to handle Slim Forte, if indeed there was a way at all.

'Please, Slim,' Rachel said, resting a hand on his arm. 'We can talk another time.'

The youthful hardcase sighed, fingered back his hat. 'What about the dance?'

'I might see you there. I'm not sure I'm going.'

He had to be content with that. Yet Forte's temper was uncertain as he flung from the building, filled saddle with one athletic bound and went storming away at a flat gallop along a street restricted by law to no pace faster than a lope.

The town was wary of this man, as it had been of many other varieties and breeds of trouble over the decades. Today they simply shrugged and went on about their business as dust engulfed the rider on the red horse now approaching the central block. There was always work to be done, money to be made and one's own business to be minded. The Wolflock man in the street had no desire to cross Slim Forte any more than he did any of the rich and often ruthless men of success who influenced and largely ruled their lives here.

Wolflock was a town where most people knew their place and adhered to the law.

Most people.

When Slim Forte got mad, and he was mad enough today, as everyone who saw him go roaring down the street like a wild redskin could testify – he tended to test the patience of citizens and the law on occasions.

The rider thundered straight by the jailhouse, raising a huge billow of dust, and when this challenge drew no response, he came racing back, the hoofs of the horse almost clipping the lip of Ike Watson's porch, so close did he come.

Still there was no sign of Wolflock's homely, diligent peace officer. And with good reason. The law office was now shut, the sheriff having decided to go off rustler-hunting in the Sweet Alice Hills, which the Mexicans called La Sierra.

Realizing this eventually, Forte cooled down some, cut his horse back to a trot and headed up-block for the Long Rail.

He noticed the dusty red horse at the hitch rail but it meant nothing to this man, who usually had a keen eye for horses, sheep and cattle – other people's horses, sheep and cattle some of his critics might suggest.

He strode inside with chiming spurs and there was a faint but perceptible lull in the murmuring sounds of the cool and shady bar-room as a result.

Men looked up from their cards, turned at the long bar,

paused in their conversations. Few Wolflockers cared for flashy and tetchy Slim Forte, yet he was not the kind of man you could ignore.

There was a muted sigh of relief when it was seen that, despite obvious signs of one of his moods, the Squaw Basin hardcase appeared polite enough as he called for a rye and mounted one of the high bar-stools without cursing or kicking the spittoons, which he had been known to do.

Forte sipped his drink and soon the drowsy mid-afternoon hum of a hot summer's day fell over the big, barn-like room. Everyone seemed peaceful, even the tall stranger seated alone at the far table in the corner nursing a cold one.

Said his name was Clint. That was all. The waitress had been tempted to enquire if it was something Clint or maybe Clint something or other, but there was a quality about him sitting there, lean and bronzed in his brown-twill shirt and riding-britches, with bronzed hands resting on the table and dark eyes shadowed, that discouraged familiarity.

The newcomer had created a brief stir upon his arrival some time earlier. His manner appeared stern and intense, and what with the cattle and sheep-rustlings and other troubles recently, well, a man could never be dead sure just whom he might be drinking next to.

But the stranger had appeared content just to sit and sip his beer, roll and smoke the occasional durham and apparently soak up the ambience of the town's finest watering-hole. After a time they almost forgot he was there and things might have remained that way but for Forte.

The hardcase was simmering down some by the time he'd ordered a second. He studied his sleek, narrow-faced image in the spotless bar mirror and did some sober thinking. After all, he reasoned, it was not as if he and Bowden's niece were keeping company or anything like that. He simply liked her style and reckoned it more than a little strange that she didn't display a more enthusiastic response to his overtures.

Others certainly did.

That thought brought a cocky smile to his reflection.

They liked a bit of wild stuff, these snooty South-western women, he mused. Especially those dark-eyed ones reared in the stuffy, chaperoned and claustrophobic confines of the standard upper-class Spanish home.

Forte had racked up some of his most memorable successes with such young women, some of whom found him almost irresistible. To an eighteen-to-twenty-year-old *señorita* reared in a straight-laced atmosphere governed by class and religion, a good-looking young hardcase with something distinctly wild about him could prove more tempting than Sir Lancelot riding up to the old hacienda on a charger of shimmering snowy white. And a lance.

Now he was scowling again.

Who was he trying to kid? Past successes or failures didn't count. He wanted to succeed with the sassy niece of Wolflock's richest citizen and would not be put off, not by her cousins, Bowden security, Bowden the man or even old Sheriff Sobersides himself.

He was a born winner. But how to win with that uppity little bitch?

He was vaguely aware of the big-breasted waitress loading a tray with a foaming glass of beer nearby, but it was not until she had delivered it to the stranger and he heard the man's voice that he swung his head in that direction.

15

The voice was quiet but deep, a big voice coming from a tall man.

Forte's stare narrowed.

The stranger with the dark hair and eyes flicked an impersonal glance in his direction, then it passed over him as though he was of no consequence.

Forte felt his neck grow hot. He was accustomed to curiosity, or at least interest and respect. Their absence here riled him. Yet there was more than that at work inside him as his gaze took in the stranger's gunrig, range-boots, the tan flatbrim resting on the table by the glass. A man in his trade must perforce be wary of strangers these days, especially should they come packaged like this. Strangers could mean trouble. Forte had been a stranger here not all that long ago, and he was certainly trouble.

The girl returned.

'Who's that?' he wanted to know.

'The tall one?'

'Who else?'

'Calls himself Clint.'

'Clint who?'

'He didn't say.'

'Everybody's got a second name.'

'Could be his surname.'

'Don't sound like any surname to me.'

'Why don't you go ask him yourself, Slim? I've got work to do.'

'Why don't I just?'

The newcomer to Wolflock didn't turn his head as footsteps approached his table. There were cool beads of sweat on his glass. He touched one with a fingertip, tasted it. The beer was just as he liked it, heady, clean and cold.

'Howdy.'

The newcomer raised his gaze slowly. 'What?'

'I said howdy.' Forte rested knuckles on the table top, blue eyes probing. 'Passin' through?'

'Could be.'

'Is that a yes or a no?'

Something changed in the deeps of Clint's eyes, something slight yet significant. 'What it is,' he said, 'is all the answer you're going to get, son.'

Forte's face suffused with vicious pleasure. This was more like it! He was getting a reaction, even hostility. It was just what he was looking for. He was still mad at the girl, so what could better serve to divert his bitter thoughts than taking it out on some stranger who plainly thought he might be something special?

'Son?' he whispered, leaning back away from the table a little and hitching at his shell-belt. 'You know, I never cared for being called that. So what are you – *daddy*? Some kind of snoop? Or a cow-thief maybe? You know we've got a whole mess of cow-and-sheep-thievin' goin' on hereabouts of late. Then again, you wouldn't be law by any chance? Well, cat got your tongue, drifter?'

Clint leaned back, the chair creaking noisily. He rested both heavily calloused hands on his thighs. All around the room, Indians, Mexicans and Americans were staring in their direction, cigars suspended in mid-air and drinks momentarily ignored as they caught the whiff of trouble.

'What'd you say your name was, son?'

'Slim Forte.' He grinned recklessly. 'I'm what you might call the *hombre* to avoid in these parts.'

Clint nodded as though soberly digesting this piece of information and weighing it for what it was worth. This was not the case. His mind was on other things and had been ever since his arrival. Although maybe he should have been doing so, he was not taking Mr Slim Forte seriously; rather the man was like a fly buzzing about the table, a vague irritant but nothing more.

'Well, son, could be the best way for me to avoid you is if you turn on your heel and get your skinny ass out of here before I bust it up some with my right boot! You savvy?'

You could hear the quiet.

The sound of a dropped match would have sounded loud as a wagon accident as Forte stood with boots wide-planted and eyes wide in their sockets, the newcomer as passive as a contemplative padre as he sat watching him. Then Forte's mouth twisted savagely and his hands were slipping close to his gun handles, dangerously close.

'Why you long, drawn-out son of a—'

That was as far as he got. For Clint had read the danger signs, and read them truly. Young, slim and hot-headed was gearing himself up to go for iron. But Clint made his play first. Next instant the heavy table was being hoisted upwards to smash into Forte, the driving shoulder beneath it powering the man backwards off his feet to measure his length on the floor, the back of his skull making brutal contact with unyielding boards.

Slim's fancy hat rolled slowly away like a cartwheel and all the shocked room could now see of the wild one were his legs and arms protruding from beneath the overturned table.

Without a word, Clint hauled the table off his man, set it upright, then collected his own hat. Forte was out cold with blood trickling from nose, mouth and eyes. The table had slammed him square in the face.

It was plain that the stranger intended quitting without a word as he walked the length of the bar, looking neither to left nor right. It was as if his thoughts were far away, and that flattening one of Wolflock's leading troublemakers had been merely a momentary diversion from whatever might be the real business which had brought him here to their town.

Or so it seemed.

Clint abruptly halted as the batwings burst apart and the law came hurrying in, eyes darting in every which direction except the corner where the unconscious man lay, with one bootheel now beginning to stutter.

Ike Watson was forty years old going on fifty. A share-cropper's son who still walked with a farmer's gait, Wolflock's lawman was dour, plodding, effective and humorless. He'd taken over the office before the coming of the railroad when things were tolerably quiet and placid in town compared to the way they were now. The job kept getting bigger and tougher and Ike Watson kept being forced into increasing his work hours. He'd been out combing the Sweet Alices for two hours today, was hot and tired as a consequence, and in no mood for trouble. Yet when he eventually sighted the unconscious figure amongst the cigarette-butts and sawdust he reckoned he'd found some, like it or not.

'You ... you did that, didn't you?' he accused the newcomer, removing his hat to sleeve away sweat, leaving a red indentation across his forehead. 'C'mon, might as well own to it, mister.'

'Weren't his fault, Ike,' called the man behind the bar. 'Slim braced him and I guess this feller just reacted before

19

the kid did somethin' foolish.'

'I'll hear it from the man's own lips, thank you, Joe Walsh,' Watson said wearily. 'Well, mister, what's your story?'

'You just heard it.'

The sheriff's face reddened.

'Now I recall, goddamnit! You're the geezer I seen banging on these doors at an ungodly hour this morning, now I get back to town to find you beating up on my citizens,' he said accusingly. 'Know what I think? I don't think you're the kind we want here in Wolflock right now, Mr whatever your name is.'

'Clint. And I'm staying on Walnut at Jackson's Roomer if you want me.'

So saying, the newcomer stepped by the sheriff and shouldered his way through the batwings. Watson hurried after him to see him untying the dusty red horse at the tooth-gnawed hitch rail. This was one chagrined badgepacker.

'Just a goldurned minute, Mr Clint!'

'Don't think much of the way you run your town, Sheriff.'

He tipped his hat and rode off down Border Avenue, leaving Ike Watson with his jaw hanging open. It was not until the lawman eventually jammed his hat on his head and stomped back inside to get a full report on the incident, that stifled laughter rose from the covey of porch-sitters at the far end of the long gallery.

'Hey, told you that drifter looked promisin', didn't I?' cackled a querulous graybeard. 'Not bad fer a newcomer, huh?' He enumerated on his fingers. 'Gits the saloon boss up two hours ahead of time, busts and hogties Forte, then walks all over Watson and tells him how to do his job. Not bad for a Johnny-come-lately, huh?'

Laughter all around. These old codgers were long past their time of influence. Mostly all they had left was tobacco, companionship and the leisure time to observe life as it flowed right on by them, and pass comment whenever it suited.

'Not bad?' responded a geriatric whose head was as totally bald as though it had never sprouted a single hair. 'It was top class. Why, I declare all the tall fella had to do was go dump Morgan Bowden tail-over-turkey, and we could award him a hundred per cent score on the welcome-to-Wolflock scale. Hey hey.'

These were light-hearted and disrespectful comments aimed at Wolflock's wealthiest and most powerful citizen, its tallest poppy. But would the words prove prophetic? Only time would tell.

# CHAPTER 2

# BAD DAY AT SPANISH RANCH

Morgan Bowden stared wistfully from the window at the enclosed wagon hard flanking the Commission House.

It was late afternoon and the curlews were calling but the Bowden sons, along with the depot hands, were still facing another couple hours of honest toil before they too might start thinking of home, whereas their father and Rachel, were already readying the buggy to quit for the day.

'Some day that'll be me, Jim,' Cole sighed. 'Start when I goddamn want, quit when it gets boring. I reckon that'd be even better than just being boss – able to come and go when you please.'

'The McQueen account.'

'Huh?'

'I need it,' stated brother Jim, rugged in shirtsleeves and plaid necktie. 'The old man wants it brought up to date tonight.'

Cole Bowden stared at his brother in disgust, was about to make a response when he heard the carriage start up. He leaned from the window and his cousin waved while his father frowned. The young man coughed on their dust and life had never seemed more unfair or arduous to this rich man's elder son. Not for the first time he'd wished he'd been born a girl. Girls seemed to get all the breaks in this family.

For many an identifiable reason, Rachel Bowden would not have agreed with this observation, had she heard it. Yet she was not about to complain about what her cousins often regarded as their father's favoritism towards her now. The rig gathered speed and she tossed her head and removed her bonnet to allow the wind to tousle her hair.

Uncle and niece shared a love for driving, especially out in the country, which was where Bowden was heading as they jounced over the planked railroad crossing and headed for South Street.

Bowden drove fast even inside the city limits. A big, flat-bellied man with capable hands and bull jaw that spoke of strength and determination, he loved the intense work at the Commission House with its ledgers and day-books and the piles of bills of lading, all pinned down by lumps-of-ore paperweights, the endless rows of pigeon-holes stuffed with yellow shipping-sheets, the huge desk which proclaimed him king of Bowden & Company and ergo, boss of Wolflock, Chavez County.

The buggy was new and fancy with ample space under the sides of the seat for the rubber-tired, brass-rimmed wheels to spin and turn with a flourish. The wheels had bright-yellow spokes. There were brass lamps mounted either side of the patent leather dashboard, and a matching yellow top that could be thrown back in the cool of the day, as it was now.

Their way led past the finest eatery in town, yet another company investment. Like most native buildings it had but one story. To the rear and south was a large patio like a hotel courtyard with a gallery running part-way round it. On occasions when the family felt like dining out they took over the restaurant and sometimes these evenings could run into the small hours with music and wine and dancing, with Morgan Bowden presiding over it all, owning it all.

He was sole owner of every company business and this was something which occasionally irritated his wife, often irked his sons. How Rachel felt about this situation he didn't know and had no desire to find out. But even if his niece considered her uncle greedy and grasping, as he knew his sons certainly did, this would not cause Mr Big any sleepless nights. He'd built the company from scratch, starting prewar and nursing, pampering and watching it grow ever since. It was all his and nobody should ever forget that fact of life.

'Believe you had a visitor today, miss?'

Rachel looked straight ahead as they approached Walnut Street.

'Yes.'

'He was his usual offensive self, so I'm told.'

'Oh, Slim is just Slim, I guess. Oh look, there's Señora Ramirez and her pony.'

'Never mind changing the subject. You know I don't want you having anything to do with that man, honey. He's bad news, I'm sure of it.'

'I don't think that's ever been established, has it?'

24

'Well, we certainly know he's been involved in a couple of shooting scrapes, and he killed that Indian over Tempest way. Besides, where does he get his money? He's always well-heeled but if he has any kind of a job then I certainly have not heard about it.'

Rachel knew Slim Forte had his full complement of faults yet she found him exciting, and nobody could deny he was handsome. But she didn't enjoy arguing about the man, was relieved when she sighted the stranger up ahead, whom she saw as legitimate diversion from their conversation.

'Oh, that must be him,' she said, pointing.

'Him?' he uncle frowned. 'Him, who?'

'Millie told me she saw this stranger at the Forty-niner. . . . My goodness, isn't he impressive.'

'Impressive?' Bowden was ready to disagree even before focusing on the object of his niece's interest. His eyes narrowed as they drew closer. The stranger stood in low-angling sunshine on the porch of the old freight depot, which had gone out of business with the coming of the railroad.

The man was tall and lean-bodied with a bronzed, clean-shaven face which seemed to have been stripped of everything not truly essential. Clean jaw, wide mouth, the kind of nose you see on the faces of Caesars on ancient Roman coins and expressive eyebrows winging back from deep-set eyes which slowly turned their way at the sound of hoofs and wheels.

Bowden's expression didn't alter as he met the flat impact of that stare. Wolflock's Mr Big was a hard man, accustomed to dealing with all types, was not about to be stared down by any no-name bum who he calculated might be lucky to own what he stood up in, his gun and maybe his horse, if he were any judge, which he knew he was.

Rachel was more sociable and less critical. She gave a small friendly smile but the stranger with his arms folded across his chest just stared at her without reaction – stared, so both imagined as the bright-yellow wheels whisked them by, just a fraction too long and hard considering they didn't know him from Adam.

'Impudent fellow,' Bowden muttered, powerful hands working the reins to take them into the final corner. 'No, don't look back, child!'

But Rachel was already twisting on her seat to study the stranger. His posture had not changed and yet she felt he was still trailing them with his eyes as though they were buttonhooks fastened onto them. Staring implacably. Strange.

'Well,' she said facing front again, 'I suppose you're proven right again, as usual, Uncle. We do seem to be attracting more than our share of strangers – and odd ones these days, don't we?'

Bowden could only nod and grunt as the rig left the town behind and went bowling out along the well-graded road which covered the five miles' run out to the company ranch.

The 'strangers' Bowden regretted most these times were the thieves busying themselves raiding his cattle and sheep. The raids were on the increase and Sheriff Ike Watson kept asking the council to recruit a couple of deputies. With typical obduracy, even though he was personally affected by the stealing, Bowden refused to approve the expenditure on additional law staff, believing that if the sheriff were doing his job properly there would not be any rustling or sheep-stealing in the first place.

The ranch rose up out of gently rolling range and Bowden used the whip.

Spanish Ranch was the big man's pride and joy, his Valhalla in the South-west. Set in the best real estate in Chavez County, the spread had once been the property of the aristocratic Belmonte family until the company sent Don Belmonte broke and picked up the 5,000-acre-spread at half its true value.

Tycoon and niece spent an hour at the sprawling adobe ranch headquarters with Rachel visiting with some of her young girlfriends while Bowden treated manager, ramrod and some of the *vaqueros* to a high-powered address on such pertinent topics as security, rustler-hunting and the like.

The sun was well down as they drove back to town. Bowden was never to be found beyond the Wolflock limits after dark any longer, even though until recently he'd traveled just as far as and when he liked, either with escort or without.

Times had certainly changed.

The railroad brought progress and with progress and prosperity came the attendant problems: strangers about town, an upsurge in crime, and overpaid sheriffs griping about the hours they must put in.

Bowden resented these restrictions imposed by his added wealth but slurped up the profits like a starving hogback hitting a melon-patch. He was a contented man and remained so at supper that night even as his sons babbled on about the news of the day, namely how a stranger named Clint had trimmed 'Rache's admirer' down to size at the Long Rail.

The name 'Clint' meant nothing to the man of affairs, but meant a great deal more to the man who bore it. In a sense, to the man who had been born and baptized James Clinton Eastman twenty-five years earlier, it meant everything.

The sheriff knew he would be late for his date tonight, just as he knew Elspeth would be sore at him. He also suspected that her mother would likely give him a piece of her mind for his tardiness – as though Elspeth weren't anything but capable of discharging that chore herself.

Mrs Spinx gave Ike Watson a royal pain in the butt. But what could a man do? Available women were scarce in Wolflock, respectable ones even harder to come by. And that went double if you happened to be a pretty plain fellow who couldn't dance to save himself and who worked the kind of hours which, if split up amongst two or three deputies, would still likely prove too much for them.

He'd inadvertently fallen asleep at the desk while taking five minutes from penning his report on the day's affairs. He'd come awake with a start to realize that the street lights were now on and he was there sitting in the dark listening to the prisoner's snores.

He grimaced, heaved his tired body out of the chair, fumbled for his lucifers.

Must have covered forty miles today, he reflected wearily, none of it easy country. The rustlers might lift stock from anyplace, yet they invariably ran the stolen stuff back into the Sweet Alice Hills which were rugged enough to hide a freight train in, if you were that way disposed. At times that day he'd felt like a lone sailor riding up one rocky swell and down the other side, cutting maybe months or even years off his horse's working life in a futile hunt for sign of those responsible for the latest fifty-head moonlight rustling raid against Spanish Ranch.

He toted his bullseye lantern in back to the little room where he fixed coffee and washed up. He stripped off his shirt and worked up a lather with his fingertips, coarse bristles abrading his skin.

Mr Bowden would not take his lack of success on his rustler-hunt kindly, he knew. Ike would attempt to explain the difficulties of being just a 'one-man band' who was often being forced to abandon his town duties in order to cover vast tracts of land alone and with little real hope of catching cow-thieves, but that would only be a waste of breath. No matter how he might phrase his complaints or explain his failures, Bowden would still light up a fresh cigar, begin pacing to and fro in one of his 200-dollar suits, rail against the thievish and ungodly and, as always, save a special slice of venom for him personally.

Ike stared moodily at his reflection in the looking-glass. Big nose, irregular features, needed a haircut, played-out and in trouble with Wolflock's Mr Big – not to mention Elspeth and her mother and the clock ticking its guts out on the Spinx mantelpiece right now.

Yet he managed a crooked smile.

For he'd never expected it to be easy, this job of working for the law along the troubled border lands of New Mexico. Why should it be? Growing up, he'd always seemed to be a day late and a dollar down compared to slick, good-looking kids whose fathers owned banks and who excelled at ball-games, swimming and horsebacking and got sent to college in Kansas before taking up careers as bankers, or industrialists.

Yet somehow the young Ike Watson had always managed to get done what needed doing in his own good time; it was no surprise that his favorite childhood story had been that of the hare and the tortoise.

He was a plugger but a dedicated one. That was one big reason for their having hired him as sheriff here, why they kept him on even though he was always griping about there being too much work for one man. It might take him twice or even three times as long as expected, but nine times out of ten he would come through successfullly on a case in the long run – with the peeping tom caught in the act; the stolen sheep found where you'd least expect; the horse-thief arrested just when everyone else had given up on ever seeing either him or the stolen nag again.

He was never – so he told himself as he wiped away the clean white lather – ever a show-pony, yet always somehow managed to be there at the finish line.

As he would be with Elspeth, despite the difficulties of which the biggest was Elspeth herself.

She was attractive in a prim-necked way, was a regular churchgoer and had had more than one eligible bachelor interested in her before the sheriff staked his claim.

She was also opinionated, skittish, tight with a dollar, overly attached to her sourdough mother and complained long and bitterly about the lawman's wardrobe and his inability to dance the waltz.

So what? he asked himself in the mirror as he plastered his dry and rebellious thatch down with a little coon-oil. She was above reproach, would make a sterling lawman's wife, and was capable of whipping up a meal capable of tempting a hermit down out of his cave and slobbering like a moose chased all day by a relay of hounds, any old day of the week.

Perfect!

The prisoner was still snoring as he hurried along the narrow passageway between the cells, these sounds now interlaced by a lighter, more ragged snoring emanating from the huge old chair in the shadowy corner by the rifle-rack where the turnkey had also found oblivion.

The sheriff of Wolflock paused to shake his head in appreciation of the irony of the situation here. The drunk had slept the day through and the turnkey had spent the greater part of it sunk in that chair alternately watching and dozing, while he himself was growing seasick riding up and down the Sweet Alice Hills beneath a raging sun astride a horse with an unkindly gait.

He sighed gustily.

He'd already done the work of three men, yet who of the three of them was now heading out into the night to tack another two or three hours onto his day? Not Drunky John or Abe Tomek, that was for sure.

In the cubicle in back of the desk and screened off by a curtain, the sheriff stripped off his sweat-stained rig and got busy dressing. The laundry woman had laid out his cleaned clothes and he climbed into them hastily yet carefully; his best white shirt, his new striped pants. He dusted off his new, too-tight star boots and with difficulty worked heat-swollen feet into them.

It took several minutes to accomplish the right degree of shine on his five-pointed star, which he then pinned carefully to his vest. With a piece of dampened cloth he rubbed away the dust from between each of the cartridge-keepers of his shell-belt and buffed his sharp-edged buckle with his coat-sleeve until it shone. He buckled on the gun, tied it down and stepped out into the office almost with a swagger.

'Raffish, Sheriff, real raffish,' he remarked deprecatingly, looking himself up and down. Then he fitted his hat to his head and headed off to do some serious courting.

Thirty minutes later Wolflock's neat if by now slump-shouldered lawman was back on the streets shaking like a ragweed in a summer windstorm.

Mother Spinx was a lucky woman, he advised himself soberly, as he made tracks for the Forty-niner Diner. A lesser man would surely have upped and belted her one with his hat for the way she went on about the ruckus at the Long Rail and his 'knuckling under' to some drifting bum who'd treated him like a hobbledehoy, whatever that might be.

That old biddy rarely left home, yet somehow always seemed to pick up the latest dirt ahead of anyone.

'How could my Elspeth possibly take seriously a beau with hair in his ears who permits nobodies from nowhere to treat him so disgracefully? And if you believe that shirt doesn't jar with that jacket, then you are sadly mistaken.'

Mrs S could combine biting criticism of one's professional life with pungent personal observations like nobody he knew. 'Hairy ears' was a new one. She was scraping the bottom of the barrel there. Then, Elspeth had surprisingly sprung to his defence. But the damage was already done. The day had been too long and the lash of that old fruit-bat's tongue had proved the last straw. He'd left with dignity and avowing his intention to get drunk. If God was good, he still might.

Heading for the yellow light of the diner, where crockery cups of moonshine whiskey were available to certain valued clients, Wolflock's harassed lawman failed to notice the figure standing in the recessed doorway next door. But Clint certainly saw him.

He fashioned a cigarette and lighted it, cupping his hands around the tobacco and paper to shield it against the high country wind blowing down boisterously from beyond Twin Bluffs, where the weather could vary from hot in winter to cold in midsummer, but where the wind blew, season in and season out.

The brief glow of the match painted his palms with gold, highlighting the callouses there, each one a testimony to the hardships of the past spent fighting the elements – sun, air, fire and water – on a daily basis to survive, and he hoped, one magic day, to succeed.

But there had been no eventual success in the Windy Hills and in retrospect he'd always known it would be that way.

He had stayed on over the hard years for reasons other than material success, was in no way surprised when it all ended with a fresh grave dug into a wind-whipped hillside upon a piece of farmland which only a masochist could love, or try to work to profit.

What had surprised him was the manner in which resentment and rage overtook him like a footpad on a darkened city street almost as the last clod dropped on the plain pine casket.

He'd not realized that he'd suppressed that side of himself for so long until he felt suddenly eager – hungry might be a truer word – to buckle on a gun and trade his plough-horse for something meaner and faster.

Something to carry him to a place imprisoned in child-hood memories as 'Wolflock ... down along the New Mexican border with Old Mexico. . . .' The phrase so often on his father's lips, especially in his last days, was now emblazoned indelibly upon his mind.

Clint took his emotions for a walk.

Passing the big lamplit windows of the Forty-niner from which drifted culinary fragrances that might have tempted and tempered any nightwalker without a cramp in his guts, he glimpsed the figure of the sheriff at his table for one, and smiled almost warmly.

He guessed he'd walked all over Watson but had not meant anything personal. He read men well; a skill you acquired over twenty years of fighting bankers, quack preachers, venal storekeepers and commission agents with hearts like shrunken baby snow-peas. Good men stood out in that harsh milieu like nuggets of gold, and he suspected Ike Watson might well be a good man.

He had to whisper to himself: 'A good man in a bad town.'

A couple emerged, a skinny well-dressed man and a very large and equally well-dressed woman. A carriage approached as if by magic. The man helped the woman climb up. She wore a vast black silk dress, big as a thunder-cloud in the skirt which was stiff enough to stand unsup-ported. She carried a dainty black-silk parasol, even by night, and wore long, black gloves chopped off at the knuckle, the latest style. This vast lady climbed into the back seat, spread her skirt, folded her hands, then glanced out to see him standing there watching. She sniffed with truly impressive disdain and they went rolling off on rubber-tired wheels leaving in their wake a vivid image of old money and elegance; no calloused palms in that family, Clint, boy.

The thought of money – old money gathering the golden moss of high interest as the years went – so dramatically in contrast with the always insufficient monies and comforts a poor family had to cope with – saw him turn his back on the central block and make his brooding way down by the railroad and the cluster of buildings along several hundred yards of the tracks, heading for where the money was made.

The slipstream from a passing switch-engine fluttered the soft silk bandanna round his throat as he lowered himself onto a pile of ties and stared up at a handsome sign informing either the locals or the passengers on the trains rolling through, that this was the headquarters and nerve-center of Bowden & Company, commission agents servicing a big chunk of Chavez County and reaching well over the border into Mexico and Sonora.

Agents were the men with brains, while producers were just the ones vulnerable to crop failures, animal plagues, rustlers, foul weather, drought and heart failure brought on by a lifetime of relentless toil.

He knew about both because his late father had been one of those who had broken his back and his heart on hard-scrabble land, yet curiously he had known the commission business backwards.

The wind grew chill but still he remained there, taking in the sturdy manifestation of one man's success which could be compared so starkly with another's failure.

He stayed until the last loco had shunted off into the big iron sheds, the wind was raising cinders and dust and there was nobody around to hear his heavy steps carrying him back to town, away from where the money was made to where it was spent.

In the far distance across the Mexican border a big storm walked off on blue bolts of lightning and was gone.

# CHAPTER 3

# WILD NIGHT
# IN TOWN

The low rumbling of heavy wheels from the direction of the river bridge heralded the arrival of men from the Font mine.

They came in every second Friday at the conclusion of two weeks spent deep underground in conditions that would shame a warthog, hacking metal out of the grudging rock and earth to cover the huge expenses incurred by Mr and Mrs Mine Boss's next wonderful vacation in the East, with the odd $100,000 set aside for a rainy day, of course.

The Font mine's drillers and shovellers and rock-buggy-pushers were a difficult, brawling bunch who hated their work. This spilled over to encompass Wolflock itself, Morgan Bowden and the law. Sheriff Watson refused to permit liquored-up Cousin Jacks free run of the town whenever they tied one on. He was ever ready to lock up any man who went too far. As a result the Fonters, as they were known here – hairy, red-faced and largely of Irish or Scandinavian origin and barbarian by inclination – invariably arrived on Fridays looking for a fight and most often finding it.

But suddenly today was looking different from other Fridays when the word reached the two big high-sided wagons crunching into Border Avenue, that the sheriff was absent. He was believed to be off chasing cow-thieves or sheep-lifters in the hills, so they were told.

The excited whooping and hollering as they jumped down to converge on the Long Rail, the Forty-niner and the Prairie Dog was enough to set doormen, bouncers, case-keepers and bartenders reaching for their billy-club batons. The scar-faced doorkeeper at the bordello actually slipped a long dagger into his cummerbund and vowed to use it should any 'hairy-assed Cousin Jack' get too rough with one of his girls.

It was probable that most of the chippies could more than hold their own against all comers – cowhands in town for a night on the ran-tan, or Cousin Jacks from the Font or visiting strangers from anyplace.

But not everyone in Wolflock was as fearless and invulnerable as the hardened lovelies at Big Julie's. As a consequence, some of the more respectable and potentially vulnerable amenities in town shut their doors upon realizing the Fonters were in and the sheriff was absent.

Bowden's Commission House was open, of course. It rarely closed. But it was noted that the regular ten-man security team had been doubled long before any hairy-faced miner had the opportunity to go check on the place with mischief in mind.

When the first Fonters showed outside Bowden's estab-
lishment, as it was inevitable that they would, they found
themselves confronted by Jim Kidd nursing a Greener
shotgun on the front landing with three of Wolflock's
more dangerous citizens posted at strategic points close
by.

Just what the miners intended doing had they found
the buildings inadequately protected was their secret. But
it was sure for certain that, whatever it was, it would not
have been anything to Morgan Bowden's liking.

Bowden owned a seventy-five per cent share in Font
mine and every man jack out there believed himself to be
underpaid and forced to work under primitive and
dangerous conditions as a consequence. The richest man
in town had a reputation for parsimony and harsh work
conditions in which he took great pride.

Some even said he'd once diddled a partner out of the
business which eventually became the Bowden Commission House.

The men settled for hurling a few epithets at the agency
staff who were looking from the windows, but moved off
compliantly enough when Jim Kidd took a couple of
experimental sightings on the ringleader with the menacing Greener.

The miner's name was McQueen, a big, rough fellow
famed for his brawling ability and tolerably well known for
the fact that Slim Forte had shot off one of his toes in an
argument at the Blue Duck two months earlier.

It said a lot about McQueen's intellect when, finding
himself frustrated in his desire to take a cut at Bowden, he
took another swig from his hip-flask and announced his
intention of looking up Forte instead.

By the time the party reached Border Avenue it comprised just one man, McQueen. The Cousin Jacks might already be half-drunk, loaded for bear and looking to make a real county circus day of this opportunity, with the lawdog missing, but not even these factors or the reassuring presence of some twenty or thirty of their dirty-face buddies were sufficient inducement for them to gear up for a possible *tête-à-tête* with Forte.

Nobody was quite sure where Slim hung his hat, or what he did for a living. But most everybody had an intimate knowledge of both his gunskills and volatile temperament.

McQueen's man was not to be found at the Long Rail but there was a temporary diversion there when Walker and Watts, two of Font's Neanderthal shovelmen, became tangled up with the saloon's bouncers, giving a good account of themselves before being thrown out into the street to a chorus of cheers, jeers and catcalls.

Wolflock's Friday was hotting up.

Three ryes and two saloons later saw McQueen's quest crowned with success when a surprisingly dirty and unkempt Slim Forte came riding by the Prairie Dog on a lathered horse. He was sucking on a short black cigar and looked no friendlier than a maverick dog wolf as he paused for a word with an acquaintance. By the time he was through, the new arrival found a big red-faced Cousin Jack standing before him blocking his way and inviting him to step down and settle things like a man, with the fists – and not with the guns, like some coward.

That McQueen was begging for it could not be denied. Even so, what happened to him should not happen to a dog. In one fluent motion Forte whipped out his pistol, heeled his horse forward and brought the weapon down across McQueen's hard head with a crack that sounded as far away as the Long Rail, two blocks distant.

McQueen struck the rough surface of Border Avenue hard, but unconsciousness didn't save him. Lashing his horse cruelly, Forte repeatedly rode the animal over the prostrate figure of the miner, steel-shod hoofs cutting him up good before Forte seemed to lose interest and calmly continued on his way.

The watching street was quiet. There was little sympathy for McQueen. Yet the incident seemed like an omen of worse to come. They'd have sent someone to look for the sheriff had they known where he might be found. But a man out looking for rustlers could be anywhere.


Ike Watson was no trailsman.

More convinced of this fact of life than ever when the faint sign he'd been following for several miles petered out altogether in a sandy gullywash, the sheriff sighed, patted his horse's sweaty neck and climbed out, looking for a shady spot.

It was hot all over the county that day but it seemed hottest here in the Sweet Alice Hills.

Watson dismounted, splashed water into his hat from his canteen for the horse first, then took a long leisurely drink himself listening to the drone of the cicadas and the slither of something scaly in the grass.

The hills stood panting all around him and the glare of light coming off yellow grass hurt his eyes. He knuckled them. Late night, last night. Thursdays he held the first of his bi-weekly line-ups; he rounded up the usual suspects, then invited citizens in to see if they might identify whichever low-down thief had stolen their milch-cow,

41

ransacked the register or perhaps attempted to interfere with the girls in the half-dark on Border Avenue.

He grimaced.

What a day to be told more livestock had vanished from Spanish Ranch! Twenty head of primes this time. The thieves were growing bolder while Bowden was growing more impatient and testier. Had it been anyone else who'd been rustled, Watson would have told them they would have to wait for a more appropriate time to have the matter investigated. You could not say that to Bowden. Nor would Mr Big listen to excuses about piled-up paper work or the problem of the Fonters coming to town, as they did every second Friday. Bowden wanted results. He believed the losses he was taking to be a disgrace, and Ike Watson had to agree with him.

The horse whickered.

The sheriff rested a hand on his rifle stock at the sound of hoofbeats, and next moment the head and torso of a rider astride a red horse showed over the clay crest off to his right.

Clint reined in and for a moment the men stared at one another across a hundred yards' sweep of dirt, shale and scrubby grass. Then the tall man clicked his tongue and the long-legged red saddle-horse carried him down the slope and across to the shade of the peppercorn tree.

'Howdy,' he said, casually as though bumping into a lawman out here alone in the wilds was an everyday occurrence. 'Find anything yet?'

Turned out he knew all about the overnight rustling. But what Clint did not reveal at the outset was the reason he was out here.

Watson felt vaguely suspicious and uneasy as he

watched the other swing to ground. This man Clint remained something of an enigma in Wolflock, impressive, remote and potentially troublesome, or at least, so the sheriff thought. What was his game? Maybe he should ask him.

So he did.

'My game?' Clint echoed, tipping back his hat to release a pool of sweat held back by the headband. He used his bandanna to swab his face, and Watson noticed the calloused hands, the scarred knuckles, the bronzed look of someone who spent his entire life outdoors. The newcomer gestured. 'Just out looking for game when I cut your sign a mile back, Sheriff. Followed it out of curiosity.'

Although he didn't necessarily believe this, it was an explanation of sorts and Ike figured he had no option but to accept it.

He said, 'Surprised to see you away from town.'

'Howcome?'

'I've a feeling whatever it is you're looking for is in Wolflock.'

Clint eyed the man narrowly.

'Who says I'm looking for anything?'

'I do.' Watson drew his tobacco sack from an inside pocket of a black coat so worn it was beginning to turn green. His eyes were shrewd but his voice was quiet as he went on. 'I'm not one of your slam-bam breed of sheriffs who shoots up all the bad guys or can track a white mink through a blizzard. The kind I am is the man who takes note of everything, tries not to forget anything important, makes his own judgements on people. You show up in my town looking big and strong enough to hold up a train. You take on maybe the most dangerous *hombre* around and

43

you come out ahead. But most interesting of all, you walk around town looking and listening, and I know there is something there you want, mean to find, call it what you will.

He licked his cigarette into shape, lighted up and drew deep.

'How close am I?' he asked.

'You interrogating me, Sheriff?'

For a moment Watson appeared more interested in the landscape surrounding them. Spanish oaks and cedars made patterns on the climbing land; here the sagebrush appeared more lavender than tan under the sun. Above the trees a range of hills as sharp as fish-teeth chopped the sky; there was little that was sweet-looking about the Sweet Alices up there. Away towards Wolflock the sky was lanced by white panels that could mean rain.

'Guess you are,' Clint said after a silence. He leaned against his horse. 'You think I could be a rustler?'

'With those hands?' Ike fingertipped a fleck of tobacco from his lip. 'I told you I'm an observer, Clint. Rustlers don't bust their guts and backs working. Few crooks do.' He looked the big man over. 'Want to tell me how you got those callouses?'

'No, I don't.'

'Suit yourself.'

'On the other hand . . . why not?'

'That's right,' Watson concurred. 'Why not?'

'Digging,' said Clint supplied, studying his palms. 'Digging for water, digging out tree-stumps, hoeing weeds, digging postholes in ground as hard as cement. Shovelling too. Years behind a plough ripping up soil that wasn't even any good as dirt, let alone for growing stuff. In other

44

words, doing it hard, lawman. Tied down on a double section of sour ground for more than twenty years on account my father was too proud to fail a second time and I . . . I wanted him to succeed.' His smile was without humor as he held up his hands palms forward. 'Every blister a story in itself.'

'You sound bitter, man.'

'Why should I be bitter?' Clint said savagely. 'Just because my father left everything behind to fight in the war . . . left my mother, his business . . . everything? Just because when he came back crooks had stolen everything from him? He lost part of a leg at Shiloh and now he had a dead wife and a kid and was expected to start all over again, and he did. . . .'

His voice trailed off. He was staring away over the dry cedars and the outcroppings of clay and gravel. He looked like a man who feared he might have said too much.

'Wounded at Shiloh?' Watson sympathized. 'You want to tell me some more about that. . . ?'

But Clint was in his saddle so fast the other could scarcely believe it. He loomed above the lawman, man and horse looking twelve feet high framed against the a faded sky.

'You do your job and I'll do mine, Sheriff!' he snapped, and spinning the red horse in its own length he went loping away. He covered some fifty yards before he twisted in the saddle to call back, 'I cut suspicious sign in an arroyo by the red cliff an hour back. Looked like horses and cattle. Could be your rustlers.'

'Much obliged,' Watson called back. 'Will you stop by Mr Bowden's and tell him I might have a lead? Might make him feel a little better.'

But Clint was gone. There was no telling if he'd heard or not. The sheriff sighed as he reached for his horse's bridle. It seemed to be getting even hotter as the day wore on.

Rachel Bowden stood beside the open window of the mansion's front room, holding the lace curtains back with one slender hand. It was coming on dark and the noise from the street was growing louder. She touched her throat to feel the quickened beating of her pulse. It had been a day of tension with brawling erupting between miners and cowboys, the long afternoon punctuated by occasional pistol shots. Almost everyone was criticizing Sheriff Watson for leaving town, although her uncle was an exception. He had virtually forced the lawman to go hunt for the rustlers, so naturally he had no regrets.

Yet the girl knew he was feeling the tension by the tone in his voice when he called to her sharply, 'Rachel, come away from that window.'

She turned. He stood before the portrait of her mother which hung over the fireplace, whiskey glass in hand, silver hair gleaming; the tycoon home from the challenges of the day.

In the wingback chair off to one side sat Elspeth Spinx, the sheriff's sometime companion and Rachel's older friend. Elspeth had come to keep her company when she'd overheard men vilifying and threatening Bowden on the streets. The woman could be fastidious and difficult, but was a true friend in time of trouble.

And Rachel had to ask herself: was there really trouble afoot tonight or was it just a case of rowdy people letting off steam?

She started at the sound of two evenly spaced shots from somewhere across town. Rachel wished her cousins were here but her uncle had ordered them off to boost the security strength at the firm tonight. Times like this made her realize just how deeply community antagonism towards her uncle really ran. She believed they hated him simply because he was so successful.

'I think we should have a stiff one, Rachel.'

She stared at Elspeth in surprise. 'But, honey, you don't drink.'

The other woman was at the drinks cabinet. 'Can you think of a better time to start?'

# CHAPTER 4

# CLINT TAKES CHARGE

Clint quit the Forty-niner and walked the noisy street. A trio of drunken miners came clomping along the plankwalk arm in arm, singing and shouting. They appeared surprised when he made way for them, for even at this early stage he'd established himself as some kind of hard man. One fellow glanced back to observe his reaction and promptly walked straight into a wooden porch support, almost knocking himself silly. His companions held him up laughingly as the reeling fellow sought to stanch the blood coming from his cut head with a bandanna.

Clint moved on, pausing on the corner of Walnut to light a small cigar. His dark eyes were watchful, his expression intent. It appeared to him that a good percentage of the men crowding the walks and flowing in and out of the saloons were either miners from the Font or cowhands from The Flats.

It also seemed that the majority of these Friday-night revelers were committed to getting drunk and heaping opprobrium upon either Sheriff Watson or Morgan Bowden – take your pick.

He had no interest in the sheriff, who appeared to be straight and maybe tougher than he looked. But the owner of both the Commission House and the huge cattle ranch was the reason he'd come south to Wolflock.

'He pays us but the bastard don't own us!' bawled a thick-necked Fonter, reeling from a doorway with one hand clutching a bottle and the other wrapped around a painted floozie. He brandished the brown bottle overhead. 'When are you goin' to pay us fair, Bowden, you Simon Legree son of a bitch?'

A Friday-night mob merely letting off steam, or something more serious? It was hard to tell at this early stage.

Clint reckoned there was an undercurrent of genuine hatred and possibly a threat of violence brewing here. Then he thought: maybe that's just how it is in Wolflock. The workers talked tough and let off steam, then meekly went back to work and did as they were told until the next time they had a skinful.

There was no concealing the universal enmity against Bowden in Wolflock. And yet, despite tonight's overheated atmosphere, he supposed that the behaviour of the workers here was not all that different from that of any other similiar town where you had one man holding all the cards and everyone else shut out of the game.

He gazed northwards.

Howcome in just about any town, most of the fine houses always seemed to be situated on the north side? he speculated. Then, shaking his head, he set out along the main street when, without warning, memory suddenly took him back in time to a tough little town in the Windy Hills region of Colorado. He was just eight years of age. That was back in the good days, long before the old man was forced to limp about with the aid of a cane.

The cow-town of Sanction was always like some glittering fantasy conjured up in the mind of a child from the country, wonderfully noisy and exciting.

That day he left his father in the lobby of one of the big hotels to conduct some business deal, and went off to investigate the stores and gimmick-shops for a time, fingering shiny items, wide-eyed at the glossy books you could buy for just a quarter – if you could spare a quarter, that was.

Gradually he worked his way west to the boozy side of town, a tow-headed country kid even then, with hardened palms from the endless chores.

This was eye-popping country to the boy's eyes. Almost everyone seemed drunk yet in no way threatening. Lurching old winos zigzagged along the walk clutching precious bottles of instant brain damage wrapped up in brown paper, or else leaned patiently against the walls waiting for people to fling away cigarette butts which they pounced on like a sparrow-hawk descending upon a fat bug.

He gawked at youths with slicked-back hair strolling by with their arms around the slim waists of pretty girls with hair the color of ripening corn – not the kind of sickly brown corn they grew out at the spread.

Every fourth or fifth building was a bar, some dim and mysterious, others rambunctious and noisy with music and laughter.

Passers-by stared curiously at a sunburnt farm kid, lean and already strong-looking in the shoulders. A painted lady wearing a vast black hat with paper flowers in the brim tried to chuck him under the chin, but he ducked and blushed. He was quick even then. Had to be to keep clear of the half-wild milch-cows out on their poorboy spread.

It was the guitar music which enticed him into a fancy place that smelled of beer and perfume. Five hillbilly musicians wearing coveralls and straw-hats were set up in back of the bar, playing music for everyone. The banjo-players strummed so fast his feet started itching, he wanted to dance so bad.

Then a swamper sighted him and shooed him out, but he could still hear that music in his head as he jogged all the way back to the hotel to collect his father at the end of his business appointment.

In those days the old man was doing well in business with a partner, and the Bell Hook ranch wasn't much more than a diversion, but one which he held onto in the event his business with his partner should go bust.

Father and son strolled the bright street together, pausing to allow a grand carriage to sweep by and catching a glimpse of the fine folk inside, smiling and laughing with beaver-coats turned up around their necks.

'That'll be us one day when my commission business with Morg Bowden really catches hold, son . . . you and me rising high and lording it over everybody. You believe that, don't you?'

'Sure, I believe everything you say, Pa.'

He'd looked up quickly to see how tall and strong his father appeared that day, an image he would long remember afterwards. . . .

Then:

'Hey, you want all the walk, buddy?'

With a jolt he realized that he was back on Border Avenue, Wolflock, and blinking into the liquor-reddened face of the miner he'd accidentally bumped.

He heard himself growl tetchily, 'Get the hell out of my way, lush!'

The man swung a weak, wild punch and Clint instantly hammered a pistoning right fist into his face with such force that the miner was belted clear across the plankwalk, from where he crashed down in the muddy street, skidding several feet in the slimed wetness before eventually coming to rest underneath a nervous tethered horse. He was out to the world.

'There he goes again,' drawled a derisive voice. 'I swear Old Hughie must be takin' tough pills, the trouble he gets into these days.' Then his mood changed as he turned on Clint. 'Nice shot, stranger,' he added sarcastically, a mean glitter in his eye, fists cocked and ready. 'Say, mebbe if you're feeling your oats you might wanna try yourself out on someone who ain't drunk or stupid?'

It was Slim Forte passing by, accompanied by a bunch of hatchet-featured men sporting plenty of artillery.

Clint was still mad. Not at the man he'd punched, or even at Forte. Mad at life and the way that final image of prospering Sanction, Colorado, had brought bitter-sweet memories.

He spat a venomous word, and the steely look in his eyes caused most of the bunch to back up.

Not Forte.

The man with narrow hips and big shoulders spun on his toe like a dancer. When he turned to face Clint again

he had both his sixguns out so fast that Clint felt his breath
catch. The cocky, arrogant face above the guns was
suddenly cold and dangerous.

'Do it, drifter!' Forte hissed. 'Go ahead and push your
dumb luck and draw, and they'll need to scrape you up to
find enough to bury. Well, what are you waitin' for? You
were smart enough when you fouled me with that table, as
I recall. C'mon, go for iron and I'll put you in boot hill
quicker than you can spit.'

Clint backed up.

He'd momentarily permitted emotion to get the better
of him. He reminded himself that the secret business that
had brought him south could of itself prove potentially
dangerous enough, without his going looking for trouble
such as tangling with a whole pack of gundogs.

Forget your pride and back down, boy, he warned
himself. Gun-punks don't count. Nothing counts but the
reason you came came down here in the first place.

Accepting his own sound advice with a nod, he
unlocked his eyes from the gunman's, licked his lips and
started off along the walk again.

Forte's jeering voice sounded as the man housed his
cutters and clapped his hands with a loud smacking
sound. 'Look, no guns now, tough monkey. So, c'mon,
let's dance the sixgun polka. You want me to put my hands
behind my back as well ? I surely will if you want, for I'm
an obliging cuss, as everybody knows.'

The man's companions were grinning. But this was
deadly serious, and Clint knew it. This man wanted to
gunfight him; that was how seriously he took their earlier
clash. He sized Forte up as vain, quick-tempered and too
cocky for his own good. But there was no way he was about

to take the other of the same breed on sight. He had to remember his real reason for being here, and it wasn't to get into gun scrapes with anybody, unless of course they happened to be connected with the man who'd unwittingly brought him here. Then he just might consider the possibility. . . .

He casually shook his head and, hands on hips, turned his back and walked off through a gaping throng.

'A yard wide across the back and every inch yeller!'

Ignoring the taunt, he kept steadfastly on and didn't look back until he had crossed the next street. No sign of Forte now. The hardcase had gotten what he wanted. Made him look scared. Maybe he had been. It didn't matter. Or at least, not yet it didn't. Right now he was preoccupied with many other things ahead of raising trouble, or trading lead for no good reason.

He was fully relaxed again by the time he was climbing the gentle slope of Border Drive and and was blank-faced and impassive by the time an armed gate-guard halted him in front of the massive iron gates of the Bowden mansion.

All the houses on North Hill were mansions, but there was one which dwarfed all the others, which he knew belonged to Wolflock's wealthiest citizen.

'I know you,' said the man with the gun. 'You're that tough guy, Clint. What do you want, tough guy?'

'I've a message for Mr Bowden.'

'I'll take it to him.'

'No dice.'

'Then get lost.'

'It's about the rustlers.'

A bulky figure stirred up on the unlit porch and Clint realized that the man had been standing there all the time.

'What is it, O'Brien?'

'Says he's got a message about the rustlin', boss.'

'From the sheriff!' Clint called, suspecting who it was.

Shadows stirred as an impressive figure stepped into the light and approached with a man clutching a Winchester at his side. That Winchester was trained squarely on Clint's chest at heart-level.

Moments later Morgan Bowden stood before him, outsized and arrogant, but impressive.

Clint felt his heart begin to trot. At last! He had last clapped eyes on his father's then business associate in the Windy Hills of Colorado when he'd been a fifteen-year-old stripling. Fifteen years since they'd last met. No flicker of recognition as the big man subjected him to a long and steady scrutiny.

'This is the geezer calls himself Clint, Mr Bowden. Seems OK, as far as we know.'

'Got a message from the sheriff,' Clint said calmly.

'Let me have it, then.'

'I reckon we need some privacy . . . Mr Bowden.'

For a moment he thought the man was going to dismiss him. Instead, he shrugged and led him up towards the great house, subjecting him to steady scrutiny from arrogant eyes.

The group entered the house and Morgan Bowden led him into a lamplit ante-room just inside the main doors.

Clint's features were impassive. But inside he was raging for reasons nobody here could even begin to guess at.

'I recall you now,' Bowden said suspiciously. 'You were watching us from the old saloon hotel yesterday. Well, what's this message you have, fellow?'

Clint quietly repeated what Watson had told him to say. Suddenly glass doors opened, revealing a bright room. He saw a slender figure approaching.

'Pay attention, mister,' Bowden said tersely.

Clint continued to watch the woman. 'Huh?'

Before Bowden could say more, Clint found himself face to face with Rachel Bowden. He'd sighted her slim figure from a distance yesterday, knew who she was. Know thine enemy? Could be sound advice.

'Uncle, what's happening. . . ?' she began, then stared at Clint. 'Oh, you're the man we saw yesterday.'

'Clint,' he said, removing his hat. 'Just Clint,' he added. 'How do you do, Miss Bowden.'

That was how it began.

Bowden very plainly wanted him to leave by this but Clint was determined to stay. He was still savoring the moment of confrontation with the man whose presence here in New Mexico was the sole reason for his being here. The man he hated and would bring down, if that were humanly possible.

After an awkward moment the rich man's niece smiled and concentrated on him, which encouraged him to turn on the charm. He eventually found himself invited inside to the drawing-room to join them in a drink, proposed by Bowden. 'To take all our minds off the unruly situation in town tonight,' as he put it.

Yet despite his words, Bowden's looks said: *How did this saddle-bum get in here?* But Rachel's smile was far more welcoming: 'I must say say you seem very different, Mr Clint.'

Clint's expression revealed nothing. 'From what, Miss Bowden?'

'Why, from the general run of gunmen Uncle seems

56

intent on recruiting in increasing numbers these days.'

The girl smiled as she spoke but Bowden plainly didn't find her words amusing. She pretended not to notice his annoyance and attempted to engage Clint in conversation. He was polite but mostly silent as he took everything in and gave very little out. This was 'Know thine enemy' time for the loner from the North.

Rachel was asking him about the 'investment opportunities' he said he was investigating here, when a sharp voice interrupted.

'And what message did he send me, pray?'

Clint studied Elspeth Spinx. Rachel's guest was fussily overdressed and sharp-featured. Her eyebrows were arched sharply upwards expectantly.

'Do you mean Sheriff Watson?' Rachel queried. 'And, by the way, this is Mr Clint from—'

'I know who he is,' the woman cut in, looking him up and down. Then she turned back to the girl. 'Of course I mean that rascally lawman. So, he visited and left again. Just like that? How very like a man. Did he happen to say when he would be back, young man?'

'Afraid not.'

'No mention of tomorrow night's dance, I suppose?'

Clint looked a question at Rachel, who was suppressing a smile. Her uncle appeared peeved.

'I suspect the sheriff has much more on his mind than dancing, Elspeth,' Rachel said, and might have said more but for the sudden stutter of boot-heels on the porch-boards outside.

'Come in!' yelled Bowden and the door swung open to admit the sentry who'd challenged Clint at the gate. 'What?'

The news was not good; 'Miners comin' up the hill, Mr Bowden.'

The smell of good leather and fine brass feathered his senses as Clint perched on a stool just inside the coach-house door, checking out the loads of his Colt .45. With the doors opened just a chink, he had a narrow longitudinal view of the front gates, a slice of the meticulously tended front garden and a section of the street.

The street below the mansions was now crowded with restless, moving figures. Five Bowden men comprising three sentries and two household staff recruited for extra duty stood, several paces apart, strung across the front lawn, rifles at the port and facing the noisy interlopers.

He'd volunteered to 'help out' when the numbers of the mining bunch came clear and Bowden had grudgingly accepted.

The situation seemed potentially explosive but Clint was calm.

For this was old stuff for the man from Colorado. Back on the tiny hardscrabble spread in the Windy Hills outside of Twin Bluffs and fifty miles from Sanction, Colorado, the ultimate irony was that, following twenty years fighting drought and poverty and his father's increasing illness and isolation, their land had suddenly become important to a realtor ready to pay big money for it, only to discover that it was not for sale at any price.

The reason was simple from Clint's point of view.

In the end, the spread was all that his father, Henry James Eastman, had left. Father and son had battled on side by side over long hard years to make it pay. They'd failed, as merciless Mother Nature intended they should.

But the old man wanted to die on his own land. He craved this to compensate for all the loss, pain and bitter disappointment that had marked his declining years. His son saw to it that, in the end, he got his final wish.

During his father's last illness, a gang of land-grabbers set out to run them off and take over the land any which way they might. The father was by then incapable of fighting, but his son was anything but unable.

Always capable with horses and cattle, Clint had learned how to protect himself and to fight during the years. His father – having gone off to the War Between The States in '61 and been pronounced Missing Presumed Dead years later – was gone. He learned to deal with every breed of land-grabber and cattle-thief: to shoot, fight with his fists, fight any which way so long as he won. Through those solitary years the youthful boss of Bell Hook ranch acquired great skill and a reputation that was set in concrete by his eighteenth birthday.

There had been the incident of the border ruffian from Missouri, a deserter from the war who came drifting west away from capture, court martial and the firing-squad. When he reached a one-man spread run by a youth, he came in with a gun with the intention of taking anything he could get his hands on and nobody had best try and stop him.

His father had left him with a repeater shotgun manufactured by Leaton & Sons, Kansas City. During the resulting skirmish with the maverick he managed to get his hands on the piece. He jerked the trigger four times, by which time the would-be looter more closely resembled a mess of slaughterhouse offcuts than the remains of a human being.

This didn't stop the scum and human detritus of the great war – many half-starved and desperate – from directing their attention to this hardluck ranch and the owner who only ever shaved twice a week.

They kept coming and he either drove them off or killed them. The spread was twenty miles from town and mostly he didn't even report the shooting incidents. He buried the losers in unmarked graves back in the woods and grew more lethally proficient with every passing season.

At war's end deserters were replaced by the criminals, nightriders, the fast guns, the snipers and the dry-gulchers. Still a man alone who had not heard word on his missing-in-action father in years, Clint, by now mature, continued to keep the Bell Hook safe for his father's return, confronting them head-on, outwitting them, killing and maiming more than he cared remember.

Until eventually they didn't come any longer; corpses rotted in the deep woods and his father came home on crutches with half a leg missing.

Henry James Eastman had been wounded at Shiloh. He had convalesced for a period, then he fell into Union hands when the Confederate stronghold was overrun: imprisoned to help rebuild the shattered South with thousands of others like him.

He survived just a couple of bad years, and it was only at the very end, suffering delirium, that the old man had unknowingly rambled on about what had really happened in his business venture with Morgan Bowden all those years ago, the injustice that had been done him.

Not a great deal of detail, perhaps, but more than enough to see Clint bury the father he loved, hire a neighbor to watch his cattle, reach the booming New Mexican border town of Wolflock with a swag of documents in his saddle-bags, a gun on his hip and a mission to fulfill.

But right at this moment, he knew he'd never expected to make this kind of progress so swiftly, getting actually to assist the man he was investigating when by pure chance a bunch of liquored-up Cousin Jacks had chosen to raise some hell.

He would make the most of his opportunity, he knew, as he leaned against the rear wheel of a Bowden carriage and scratched a vesta into life upon a Bowden stanchion.

He had learned a great deal about the enemy in his short time here, he realized. As well as ongoing strife with the miners the rustling raids on the giant spread had eaten into Bowden profits and, characteristically, the big man had set out to cut costs to compensate. This pruning entailed a ruthless cutting of wages and salaries paid to his many employees in Wolflock, upon the huge Spanish Ranch, at Font mine and at the mainstay of his empire, the Commission House.

This trouble here in town had been brewing a long time. With Ike Watson absent today, it had come to a head.

A deep-voiced Greener shotgun blast sounded and Clint moved to peer out. Smoke drifted from Jim Kidd's rifle over by the fountain of the mansion house.

'That was a warning!' the security boss from the Commission House shouted at the concealed enemy. 'Now git gone or git hurt!'

A flung rock sailed over a fence to shatter paving stones close by Kidd's position. And now miners were shaking the big steel gate. You could almost smell the beer and cheap whiskey from the coach-house.

Clint whirled as a door opened in back. He went low but straightened slowly upon making out the slender, white-garbed figure of the niece.

'Over here,' he hissed. 'What is it?'

Rachel approached hesitantly. 'I came to see if . . . if you were still here.'

'Now what sort of a dumb thing—' he began, then paused. 'Just a minute. Whose idea was this? Yours or your uncle's?'

'Mine.' She twisted her hands together. 'You see, I was growing rather nervous up at the house and I . . . well, somehow I sensed I might feel safer knowing you were still out here. That must sound like a strange admission, you being almost a stranger, but that's the way tonight.'

The tightness left his face. She was not guilty of anything, he reminded himself. Maybe the mission he had set himself was doomed to failure, buried beneath the weight of the years.

'It's all right,' he said, putting his arm about her shoulder and giving her a reassuring squeeze. 'Come on, sit with me over by the doors and we'll see if the circus is still in town.'

It was. And now a group of grimy figures was pushing its way through the open gates onto Bowden property.

'I hope you folks don't fun it like this all the time down here on the border, Rachel?' he said, trying to make light of it for her sake.

'We seem to have nothing but trouble lately. All our workers are so discontented.'

'You think they might have reason?' Clint spoke slowly. He was watching a hairy-faced figure in miner's denim sidling away behind the shrubbery on the far side of the immaculately kept lawn looking jittery.

'Perhaps.'

He was surprised by her response but before he could respond he sighted the sidler emerging from the shrubbery in back of Kidd's position. The man was clutching a length of lead pipe.

This was getting serious.

He stepped out in the open with gun in hand, and shouted: 'Back up, you men. You're trespassing on private property! And you, I'd drop that pipe quick smart if I was you!'

He looked tall and commanding and held a naked blue Colt in his fist. The miners at the gates hesitated but the plug-ugly clutching the pipe must have fancied his chances. He let fly with his weapon which arced end over end towards an unsuspecting Kidd. It struck him in the middle of the back and drove the man gasping to his knees. The ragged cheer from the gates was suddenly swallowed up by the arrogant bellow of a Colt .45, and the pipe artist was turning ash-gray as he clutched a thigh with both hands and fell backwards into a shrub.

A plume of silent smoke rose from Clint's gun barrel.

That should have finished it, but didn't.

The miners had been working up to this for weeks and had enough liquor aboard to hone their fighting spirit. The wounded man was their leader. They exploded into drunken fury and surged forward *en masse*. Clint was now seeing the animal face of a mob, one of the ugliest sights on earth.

It was nothing new for a man named Clint.

He'd lost count of the number of times he'd faced down intruders, sometimes singly, often in numbers, back in snowy Colorado. He didn't want to kill anyone here tonight, but he had a powerful personal reason to protect Bowden that no citizen or wild-eyed miner could possibly imagine.

The mob was roaring and raging but there was no sign of anyone threatening gunplay as yet. This was encouraging. Colt cocked and ready, Clint moved deliberately towards the trouble to reach the stones well before the first rioter could reach that half-way mark.

The drunken figure in miner's denim charged at him like a range bull only to be knocked cold with one sweeping cut of gun barrel.

The mob howled in rage, yet their progress had slowed, which the man with the .45 noted. But just as swiftly the mood changed again and they were coming forward in bunches, brandishing batons and staves and urging one another on.

Taking command of the moment, Clint took several long-legged strides forward and attacked a bunch of three with the barrel of the Colt, which rose and fell like a timberman's axe, cracking skulls and battering limbs. He was like a farmer at work, scything down a ripened crop, but what ploughman ever toiled with such brutal efficiency?

A single husky brute came charging headlong from the by now stationary main mob only to be smashed down into Bowden's smoothly raked gravel drive face first, with crimson running from his broken mouth, one arm twisted under him at an unnatural angle. Clint's gun back on full cock, he called across to Kidd while holding the mob steady with his eyes.

'You know them?'

'I certainly do.' The speaker was Bowden, now joined on the gallery by his sons and Elspeth Spinx.

'You'll all face the sheriff when he gets back,' Clint told the rioters, sounding exactly like a lawman himself in that moment. The gun barrel flicked. 'You've got ten seconds to disappear.'

They were gone in less time than that, scuttling away and glancing back wonderingly at the tall figure silhouetted against the house-lights. It was a rout more than an honorable defeat – how could one man's triumphing over maybe a score be anything else? Sobered and bitter-faced, the workers began squawling amongst themselves, just like angry dogs, stung by another defeat and humiliated by the manner in which it had been dealt them. The Bowden party, by contrast, was gratified yet puzzled, none more so than Bowden himself. And each one was asking the same question.

Why should a man whom they barely knew take such risks on their behalf?

It seemed a reasonable question but they were not destined to receive any kind of explanation. At least not yet.

# CHAPTER 5

# RUSTLERS' ROOST

The scarred and battered sign above the doorway of the last building in the gloom of Shotgun Alley read indistinctly:

BURGE, BURGE, CLACKETT & BURGE:
ATTORNEYS AT LAW

The night-caller hesitated, as well he might. He'd been warned that the firm he considered calling upon was 'doing it hard', but this seemed ridiculous. Maybe he would do better to consult one of the far more impressive law offices up along the main street.

Then, scratching his head, he reminded himself that there was good reason for seeking legal assistance away from the bright lights and well-to-do clients. The way he figured, an attorney doing it tough would be far less inclined to be on a retainer from the Commission House or its owner, Morgan Bowden.

A tomcat snaked past, hissing. That did it. He turned to

go back down the rickety steps when the scarred old door was flung open, a flood of sickly yellow light engulfed him and a figure stood on the top stoop, clutching a stave.

'All right, you mangy little sons of bitches – huh? Who in hell are you?'

Clint studied the man. He was small and skinny in an ill-fitting black suit with an enormous celluloid wing collar sticking up around his ears. His complexion was hectic while his mood appeared at least borderline violent.

'Er . . . Mr Burge?' Clint said hesitantly.

'Clackett. What's your business?'

'Er, I'm not sure—'

'Then get off my stoop and off my street until you are sure. . . .'

The voice faded as the Dickensian figure leaned forward. 'Say, aren't you that new gunslick that's been sucking up to that arch-bastard up on Snob Hill? Sure you are. I saw you kick a defenceless citizen off the Days of Glory front step yesterday—'

'That citizen had just stolen a kid's snack-money. But do I understand you are no great friend or admirer of Mr Bowden of the Commission House, Clackett?'

'Mr Clackett to any crummy gunslick-cum-Bowden-suck. So, what the hell do you want?'

'Are you free?'

'To do what?'

'Why, free to consider a commission, maybe.'

'Commission?' the other echoed. He licked dry lips as though he was tasting the word commission, slurping it up. He grimaced fiercely and only belatedly did his visitor-cum-client realize that he was smiling as he bowed, stepped aside and waved Clint in with an expansive gesture. 'Son, you've come to the right place. Get inside so I can shut this door before someone throws a dead cat through it.'

It was an inauspicious beginning which quickly showed signs of improvement when both men were seated on opposite sides of a reasonably tidy desk in an at least moderately respectable, if undersized office.

Studying his man, Clint was almost reassured. The attorney had seemed eccentric before, now he merely appeared unusually intense and excessively authoritative as he growled, 'All right, don't waste my time. Talk!'

Clint talked, but certainly took his time. Probing the man's attitudes, affiliations, prejudices and eccentricities, it may have taken him a quarter-hour before he was satisfied with two things. One, that the attorney was a sworn enemy of the Bowdens, and two, he appeared to be a man of integrity, as he had been described by several citizens uptown.

Clint rolled a durham and took the first good draw before placing his cards on the table. They were major cards. His late father had been a business partner with Morgan Bowden in Colorado pre-war. He had suspicions bordering on certainty that Bowden had taken advantage of Henry James Eastman's long absence both on military service and as a Union slave-laborer for a considerable period post war.

'My father is dead and there's nothing I can do to bring him back,' he concluded, lifting a leathern documents satchel from the floor and placing it atop the desk. 'I reckon he was somehow tricked, cheated or perhaps even forced from the partnership, which Bowden eventually brought down here to Wolflock with great success. I want you to examine these documents, come to a conclusion, and if your angle on what happened to my father jells with mine . . . well, I'll take it further from there . . . if the time comes.'

Silently Clackett fingered through the fat wad of documents, frowned, lighted up a pipe, leaned back and gusted smoke at the nicotine-darkened ceiling.

'You loco or something, boy?'

Clint scowled. 'What?'

'Ever hear of a woodchuck winning a ruckus with a grizzly?'

'Don't beat about the bush, damnit. Yes or no, and make it fast!'

Attorney Clackett cracked a grin for the first time.

'Well, you got spirit, that's for sure. And you can handle yourself, the whole town's talking about that. But you still look like a woodchuck in grizzly country. Well, I'll take it on, greatest of pleasure, mainly on account nothing would please me more than to see that bloated big-noter pay for what he's done to the folks of this county, the little folks.'

He paused, stabbing the fuming cigar in Clint's direction.

'Only thing, if the big man gets wind of what you're up to and they find you in an alley one morning with a bullet in your back or your throat cut, don't come blaming me? Understood?'

'Understood.' Clint smiled, and they shook.

The shot that startled them came from somewhere to the riders' right, from the moonshadowed nest of granite boulders resembling giants' marbles on the slope above the trail.

Buell gasped as the report was engulfed quickly by the drumbeat of hoofs. He heeled away from the stampede line of baldy-faces, his eyes raking the boulders, sixgun in hand as he closed on his man lying face down in the grass. One glance was all it took to know his man was dead. But how could this be? The rustler's boss had planned the biggest strike yet against the Spanish Ranch herds right down to the last detail. He had the position of every Bowden nighthawk pin-pointed, or at least he believed he did.

The bunch had lifted the stock smoothly, quickly and silently and were counting themselves as good as home by the time they'd quit Spanish Ranch dirt to make their headlong way along this animal-pad trail winding off into the Sweet Alice Hills. They were confident that nobody would be posted away out here. As far as he knew, Bowden had most of his men on town duty tonight in the wake of the violent incident at his mansion.

Buell twitched as the sniper opened up again and something whipped past his horse's face, damn near clipping his knee.

He identified the sharp spang of a Spencer carbine, a different sound from the first shot.

More than one man up there. Could be a whole bunch!

Ripped-up clods of earth rose and fell in his wake as the lean-bodied gunner galloped off after the fast disappearing cattle at full stretch. Big-nosed Buell was all class when it came to rustling, yet barely rated when it came to gunplay. That was the reason he would only ever work supported by top gunmen. Men like the lithe-hipped figure astride the mouse-colored mare he found waiting for him in the beech shadows dead ahead now.

'Who in Sam Hill is shooting at us?' Slim Forte's voice was taut with tension as Buell slewed to a halt by his side, blue eyes cutting to a single gleam as he stared back at the beetling rocks.

'Someone who can throw lead, is who, boss. Jake's done for.'

Forte swore softly. He had no tears for a dead henchman. Nor was he concerned if his gang was being forced to whip their stolen beeves at a dead run right along the secret hill trails at that very moment. The worry that griped his guts was that the rules of the game had plainly changed. Bowden was getting craftier and cleverer by the day and plainly had figured that they might use this runout route next time they struck his fat herds, and so had taken precautions against that eventuality.

Those dumb-ass miners had got Mr Big all stirred up, and now *he* was paying the price!

'Whoever's yonder over there in them rocks knows which way we're headin',' he said, mouth cut to a razor slash. The ice-eyes cut to Buell's pocked features. 'Which means we can't afford to let 'em report back to Bowden.'

Buell gulped audibly, catching his drift.

'Jeeze, Slim, there's only you and me agin' God knows how many of them up yonder. And remember what we heard after our last raid. The word was that Bowden was shippin' in extry nighthawks and doublin' homestead sentries since the miners' big play and—'

'Let's ride, Irvine.'

'But, pard—'

'You ride decoy down along the trail.' Forte's curt voice drifted back as he heeled away up through the scattered timber. 'I'll get in behind 'em.'

That was the plan. Buell knew it could work if Slim said so. And were he forced to make a wager on the outcome of the looming gun clash, he would bet that his deadly partner would survive. What brought him out in a cold sweat and had him looking more like a wino trembling in the grip of the delirium tremens than any kind of rugged rustler as he drove his horse back into the moonlight, was wondering if *he* would stay alive.

He gnawed at clenched knuckles.

Acting as decoy for anybody – even for a gunner like Forte – could be a damnably risky business, he knew only too well. That rule applied even to decoys with guts and gunspeed, and he didn't shine on either of those levels. He was a damn good rustler, period. And this rustler cursed when he realized he'd made his knuckle bleed. . . .

But orders were orders, and must be followed. He headed back in the direction of the distant spread, along a dim trail barely out of rifle range of the boulders, as a mouse-colored horse flitted through dappled moonshadows a half-mile above him.

In sharp contrast to his nervous henchman, Forte was the iceman on horseback as he guided his mount through the timber.

He stiffened sharply upon glimpsing furtive movement within the nest of hulking boulders some distance ahead. He instantly reined the prad back a little and instinctively selected the soft footing where hoofs made little sound. He nodded in sly approval at the sounds of Buell's cayuse raising a ringing clatter from the flinty surface of the trail below. Good diversion from himself. His Colts went in their holsters now. He abruptly jerked the saddle carbine from its scabbard and slid from the saddle, deftly looping the reins over a low bough.

An uneven line of lesser rocks and tufting brush ran down from the treeline almost to the scatter of granite boulders below.

Crouched low, he began working his way down. Suddenly two shots rang out and gunsmoke spewed out from the ancient stones. But no hot lead came flying about his fast-moving form. They were firing upon Buell, who was out of range still. Or so he hoped.

No return fire came up from the trail. Buell was supposed to keep shooting to keep the ambushers occupied. Forte knew the rustler was either down or dead. His instincts told him so, and they were rarely wrong.

He gave up on stealth and concentrated on speed now, knowing it wouldn't take long for the snipers to figure out that Buell's role had had to be that of a decoy, and designed to protect someone else.

Him.

Slim Forte was as fast as they came and a twenty-yard downhill dash culminating in two giant leaps saw him dive headlong for the closest boulder in the cluster before the first suspicious head was raised.

Sliding like a big hitter coming home to base, the gunman used the carbine one-handed to blow a hole in the look-out's head, the smashing impact of the heavy-nosed slug flinging the man's whole body back as though clipped by lightning.

'Hey! You OK, man?'

Deep in the rocks now, Forte tracked towards the sound of that urgent voice. He looked every inch the ice-cool killer now, every nerve and instinct geared for the next lethal play of arms.

Times like this Slim Forte had to believe it was all worth-while, that his long-term plan to undermine Bowden's power through ruthless plundering of his herds, whilst at the same time adding to his own financial strength and stature from the outcome of the selling-on of the stolen cattle, would be successful. All this simply had to be worth risking his neck for every so often as he was indeed doing right at that second.

For far too long before coming to Chavez County this badman's life had seemed a pointless whirl of gunsmoke, women, dope and excitement. Ambition didn't hit until the day he came face to face both with Bowden's bloated wealth and arrogance – and, of course, the man's high-bred niece.

Once real ambition grabbed him by the short hairs, the gunman was amazed by what he was capable of: organize a high-grade rustler gang; curb the wildness in himself which so often landed him in trouble; pursue a course that reached far beyond those old youthful, easier goals of the next kill or the next woman. He found that he could handle it all.

He was convinced that if a man wanted something badly enough he must be willing to die for it. And depend-ing upon whom or what he might be stacked up against here, this could easily prove to be his dying-time, should he make just one slip.

And dying-time it was. But not for Slim Forte.

Bowden's newest signing was a middle-aged gun profes-sional who'd made the error of underestimating just what he was up against. Having sighted Forte's slim figure at a distance, he'd merely figured himself to be up against nothing more than some breed of wild gunkid. So he expertly flipped a pebble over Forte's position, waited a split second to give the man time to turn in that direction, then came charging around a gray granite boulder with both guns blazing.

Forte had not turned away. The carbine spewed purple shot gunsmoke and yellow flame, and in one crimson instant, the night, fifty head of primes and the honor of victory all belonged to Slim Forte. Too bad about Irvine Buell.

It was the hour before dawn before the lone rider raised the massive stone pyramid of the Sierra Espantoso, or Frightful Mountain. With the killing behind him and the certainty that the gang would run the cattle through to their crooked beef-buyer over at Phantasm Canyon without any hitches, he saw no reason to hurry and so took the leisurely route back via Mile High Trail.

This was in the very heart of the Sweet Alice Hills where towering ramparts fanged the dark sky and where ancient volcanoes had flooded vast sections of the hills' inner keep with lava so dark and glossy that it looked as if it had cooled but the day before.

Below the Mile High lay a nightmare world of draws, arroyos and chasms, crossing and criss-crossing, interlocking in hopeless mazes and bristling with impenetrable forests of catclaw and jumping cholla, crucifix thorn and wait-a-bit bush.

These lower regions were thick with every breed of venomous reptile, ranging from the deadly Sonoran coral snake up to sidewinders and clusters of thick-bodied diamondbacks.

This land was like him, he reflected: hard, cruel and

unforgiving. But unlike himself, the ironically named Sweet Alices were not going anyplace. Since the ambition bug had bitten him his life had changed totally. Everything was for a purpose now, and he no longer went off half-crazy and half-cocked the way he used to do whenever the wind blew against him.

He was mature now, a force to be reckoned with.

Or so he believed until he reached the hideout to hear a report on the successful sale of Bowden's beef, and to catch up on the latest from Wolflock from his spy in that man's town.

The spy was smart. He'd trawled up plenty of valuable information including details of the showdown with the miners at Bowden's mansion. He had even been privy to some lighter kind of chit-chat which his eavesdropping ear had scooped up concerning Slim's antagonist, Clint. He said he had it on good authority that that high-stepper was rumored to be escorting Slim's hoped-for sweetheart, Miss Rachel, to tonight's Summer Ball.

Forte's hawk-face turned to granite.

He stared hard at his man across the camp-fire, small flames lighting his predatory features. He knew the rat-faced little bastard had deliberately slipped in that snippet just to see how he would react. The old Slim might have bitten like a big-mouth bass, he knew. But not this new serious player that he had become in the county. Outwardly he remained calm and casual as he issued final instructions. That done, he had someone saddle up a fresh horse which was soon carrying him back along the Mile High, pushing west.

He waited until Frightful Mountain vanished in back of him before taking out his guns and blowing apart a fat adder that had been watching from a trailside rock. The small kill eased the anger burning his guts a little. Yet he was still far from the cool man in full command of himself and the situation as he kicked the animal into a mile-eating lope.

Ike Watson never slept late. Reared on a farm where the people woke the roosters instead of the other way around, he'd never fallen into the lazy habit of lolling in until six o'clock or so ever since the day he first pinned on a badge and got to be virtually his own boss.

Even so, it was hard getting out this Saturday morning, and he felt even lousier when he remembered the news that had come in late last night before he could get to bed after spending most of Friday in the saddle. There'd been another raid on Spanish Ranch while he'd been out futilely hunting leads on the previous raid.

Fifty head run off and two hands killed in the process!

In urgent need of soothing caffeine, he might have brewed up a powerful mug of bad coffee right now, had it not been his long-time custom always to have his first down at the jailhouse. The sheriff was a man of routine in a job where routine was getting harder and harder to maintain.

He stepped out into the cool gray morning and instantly felt better despite a certain saddle stiffness and a touch of sunburn.

Down the street he could just make out the high bulk of the hotel, lightless and asleep; the whitewashed walls of Old Town adobes were ghostly blobs across the silent train tracks.

He started off.

A few stars still burned but almost as soon as he looked up at them they were gone.

This was the best time of day, everything clean and fresh. He walked past the hotel and the row of empty rocking-chairs along the gallery. Hands thrust deep into his pockets, he could see the light strengthening to the east, outlining the high, clean lines of Bowden and Company's looming Commission House.

Good business, the commission business, he reflected with just a flicker of envy. And simple. You bought, sold, handled, transported and fixed a price on everything – and skimmed off a fat commission on it all down to the last grain of oats.

And, naturally, you made certain nobody else in your bailiwick ever got to act as a commission agent.

Was he envious of Mr Big?

Sure he was. But he still wouldn't change places with Morgan Bowden. He had more enemies than Custer would encounter attending a Sioux burial.

He refused to consider how mad Bowden would surely prove when he showed up at the office today, and he *would* come. Miners attacking his home while rustlers attacked his herds and killed his men – all on the same night? Who wouldn't be sore?

Yet he went on enjoying the strong sense of possession and responsibility that was his each new morning and which sometimes could last all day.

He would not feel guilty about the current level of crime. He was understaffed and under-supported. Maybe that was all part of being a town sheriff. But it could be that today would be the day when something unexpected might be handed to him on a platter, some lead, hint or clue that could lead him triumphantly to solve what he could only accurately call 'the Bowden troubles'.

He paused at that thought. Seemed Morgan Bowden was never actually trouble-free these days, and jailhouse records showed that this had always been so. Could the big man's propensity for greed, aggression, manipulation and oppression of the poor and the weak, along with his deep-rooted unpopularity, have something to do with that situation?

The sheriff of Wolflock propped. Ike Watson looked round almost guiltily as though fearful that someone might be around who could read his thoughts. He half-grinned as he moved on. He was not afraid of Bowden, but his job did require that he maintain good working relations with 'Mr Big'. Seemed nobody in the town ever had the gumption to defy the man openly, unless it happened to be some underpaid miners, or Titus Poole's wild cowboys from the Flats.

By the time the turnkey showed up at eight the sheriff's morning was well under way. Leaving the man in charge he set out upon his first patrol of the day, which seemingly inevitably led eventually to North Hill and the mansion.

Armed guards manned the gates.

He got the story on the overnight troubles from these men, and came to realize just how dominant a role the man named Clint had apparently played in the incident. This both pleased and troubled him. He was grateful that someone had taken on those drunken Cousin Jacks in his absence, yet Clint's violent participation stirred a vague unease.

Just who and what was that fellow, and howcome he was buying into Wolflock's troubles anyhow? The sheriff liked to pigeon-hole people but Clint didn't fit neatly into his filing system. This could be merely his imagination, yet from the outset he'd seemed to detect something driven and potentially dangerous behind that bronzed mask of a face and the deep, dark eyes.

Bowden caught him before he could escape. This gobbled up a half-hour. The rich man was outraged and wanted to prefer charges against every single miner between here and Santa Fe.

The sheriff was astonished to hear himself interject: 'Nobody likes to have their wages cut, I guess, Mr Bowden. All that hooraw and trouble could be as simple as that simple fact of life, don't you reckon?'

Bowden reared back on his boot-heels, visibly shocked. 'Are you implying this outrageous incident was my fault, Sheriff Watson?'

'You heard anything further on the stolen cattle?'

He was switching the subject, and it worked. Bowden proceeded to fulminate against the cow-thieves who seemed to have designated Spanish Ranch as their prime target of the summer. Last year the Commission House had been battling with the railroad, the year before Bowden was suing fellow-ranchers over water rights all across the county.

Next year?

He wouldn't put it past the big man to take on the New Mexican government if he didn't care for the way they were running things. Hard, grasping, ruthless and supremely arrogant, that was Morgan Bowden. And Ike Watson felt a surge of relief when the sons emerged from the house dressed for another full day at the office. Bowden employees worked six days a week, sometimes seven.

He liked the boys and they liked him. Soon the three were chatting easily, and eventually Bowden gave a snort and stamped inside, yelling at the servants.

'You're going to have to nail those rustlers or we'll have to put up with Dad's filthy mood indefinitely, Sheriff,' said Cole with a wry grin.

'Or at least keep Rachel away from strange men,' laughed Jim.

'Huh?' Ike said, not understanding.

'He's sore about that, too,' Jim explained. 'Sitting around here talking after the Cousin Jacks were sent packing, this Clint feller upped and invited Rache to go to the ball with him. She said yes and Dad has been spitting chips ever since.'

'Which reminds me, I don't really have a date for tonight,' said the sheriff in his easy way. He flipped his hat and caught it. 'See you boys tonight, I hope. And I'll keep working on the rustling.'

But neither missing stock nor rampaging miners clouded his thoughts as Ike Watson retraced his steps down the long town hill. He was thinking about Elspeth and her difficult ways, about her mother whom he would like to pack off east to the abattoirs with the next shipment of beef-cattle. In particular, he fantasized how much he'd give for one full week away from the streets, locked up in some sleazy hotel with Elspeth and a big brass bed.

He knew what that woman badly needed, and it wasn't maternal advice about him and his shortcomings.

As he swung into the avenue he sighted the store-keeper's roustabout sweeping the boardwalk in front of the store; when the man saw him he stepped up his stroke in a burst of animation. A battered mine-wagon was rumbling his way with several badly battered faces staring down at him over the high sides.

'Hey, Watson, have you done your duty and arrested that long bastard for what he done to us last night?' shouted Watts, of that troublesome twosome Walker and Watts. 'Jest take a look at us. Bruises and cuts all over. Just what sort of a burg are you runnin', anyway?'

'I'd jug the lot of you if I had the time!' Watson called after them. He didn't mean it and they knew it. They were like big tousle-headed children in his eyes, implusive, violent but somehow almost like innocents. They were not his main problem these days, more like simple irritants.

Glimpsing two skirts disappearing into the millinery, he removed his hat, slicked down his hair, brushed a speck of dust off his rig and followed them inside.

He found Rachel Bowden and Elspeth at the bonnet counter. The women smiled a greeting and he squared his chin and strode right up to them. Time to be a man? There would never be a better.

'Elspeth, about this damned dance tonight—'

'Why, I'd love to go with you, Ike.'

He stared, mouth hanging open. 'Er . . . you would?'

'Of course,' Elspeth beamed, taking his arm. 'Rachel is attending with a perfect stranger, so she will need chaperons, won't she? I shall be ready at eight sharp. Do try not to be tardy, there's a dear.'

He quit the store fast before she could change her mind. Women! He was ready to jail any man for life who professed to understand them. So why should he worry what it was that had caused her to make this decision? She was going with him – that was all that signified. Now he'd better get a neck trim at Alfonzo's.

There was one empty chair at the hairdresser's, one occupied. Very much so. He didn't realize who was getting shaved until Clint spoke. 'Morning, Sheriff.'

Watson immediately had to thank the man for last night. He readily conceded that the whole affair could have been a major disaster but for his intervention. Maybe even someone killed, perhaps. As it was it was there had been just one miner wounded and a half-dozen pistol-whipped. 'I could use a deputy like you, son,' he said honestly, settling back into the vacant chair. 'First you give me a lead on the rustlers, then you pull Mr Bowden's irons out of the fire for me. One I owe you.'

'No luck with the rustlers, so I hear?'

Ike's honest face tightened as he shook his head.

'The sign petered out. Then the bastards hit again and later gunned two of the Spanish's green nighthawks.' He sighed and settled deeper into the cushions. 'Yessir, he's sure as certain in the wars these days, is Mr Bowden.'

'A lot might say he has it coming, Sheriff.'

Watson met Clint's eyes in the mirror as the tall man rose from his chair. The dark eyes were flat, implacable. The lawman stirred uneasily under that hard stare for a moment.

Then he said, 'I'd like to think of you as a friend of the law, son. You certainly acted like one yesterday. Just hope I'm not wrong, is all.'

'I believe I'm one hundred per cent right about a few things here in your town, Sheriff,' Clint replied enigmatically, putting on his hat and making for the door. 'But for your information, I'm on my way to confirm this fact one way or another right at this moment, as luck would have it.'

Watson's frown followed the tall figure across Border Avenue and into the mouth of South Street, where he saw him pause in front of a doorway before going in.

'Curious,' he muttered, settling back while Alfonzo draped a striped towel about his neck and tucked it into his collar. 'Now what would a feller like that there want with the attorney at law?'

'The usual, Sheriff?'

'Yeah, the usual. . . .' He was dozing before the barber got properly started.

He needed all the rest he could get. He sensed this was going to be a big night.

# CHAPTER 6

# ECHOES OF
# THE GUNS

The brass plate alongside the redwood door read;

R. BACA-BROWN
Attorney At Law. Legal Advice and Counsel.
Collections Made. Loans Arranged. Mortgages.
All Instruments of Writing
Promptly Attended To.

Clint sniffed the musty air as he entered the chambers of Wolflock's premier attorney at law. From behind an ancient desk rose an ancient figure, dark of complexion, white of hair and piercing of eye.

'Hmm, Mr Clint, the mystery man and enforcer, or at least, so I am led to believe. How do you do, sir?'

Clint accepted the papery handshake, his surprise showing plain.

'You know about me, Attorney?'

'It's an attorney's duty to know all things about all men if possible,' the man said, with a whiff of irony, waving to a high-backed chair. 'What can I do for you?'

Clint's features hardened as he sat and pulled off his hat. 'Maybe the hardest thing possible. I'm here to ask you to tell me the truth. Or, could be I'll insist on it.'

His tone was even but the faint hint of threat was unmistakable. Attorney Baca-Brown, whose shingle had hung outside this grand adobe building since the fifties, leaned back in his hand-carved Spanish chair, placed the tips of his fingers together and eyed his visitor warily.

'If we are going to be honest with one another I suggest you start by furnishing your full name – Mr Clint.'

'I'm James Clinton Eastman.'

The attorney scribbled the name down on a piece of paper, frowned at it as he held it up. The sharp old eyes flicked up at Clint, who said, 'Ring a bell? I'm the son of Henry James Eastman.'

Baca-Brown had presided over matters legal from this room above the street for thirty years. The man was tough, able, shrewd and reputed to be honest. All this Clint had gleaned from the locals, who in general respected the man, some displaying both affection and gratitude for past services.

But the fact about Baca-Brown which interested him most was that he was known to have been Morgan Bowden's personal attorney at law for a large slice of those thirty years. The man had also once performed certain legal services for his late father, late of Windy Hills, Colorado.

The attorney made to rise.

'I'm not at all sure I can help you, Mr Eastman—'

'Sit, old man!'

'I warn you that I shall not tolerate offensive or coercive behavior, young man. I'm suggesting you leave or I shall summon the law.'

'You gave Bowden all the sweet time in the world twenty-five years ago and you'll give me all I want unless you want to wind up behind bars at seventy years of age for fraud and abuse of privilege.'

He'd done his homework long before coming to this place. He was as implacable as a hanging-judge, and the old man was shaking a little as he slowly resumed his seat.

'What . . . what are you talking about?'

Clint told him.

Twenty years ago. . . .

Commission agent partners Eastman and Bowden were doing modestly well in their fledgling business in Colorado when Henry Eastman heeded the call from the front and accepted a commission in the Army of the United States.

The necessary paperwork governing the continuing operation of their joint business was, during Eastman's absence, entirely handled by Bowden and concerned the legal aspect of a young and prospering business. Subsequently matters were handled by Attorney Baca-Brown, operating on behalf of both partners.

There had been, however, as Eastman's son was to discover much later, no provision made for him were his widowed father not to survive the war.

And in the smoking aftermath of the Battle of Shiloh, the report came through both to Colorado and Wolflock, where Bowden had shifted to set up his greatly enhanced business empire by that time, that Captain Eastman was missing in the action, believed killed.

One year later with the professional able assistance of Attorney Baca-Brown, Morgan Bowden filed suit before the 14th District Court of Santa Fe to have Captain Eastman declared legally dead. This was duly granted, at which point the presiding judge deemed that in the absence of a will or documents to the contrary, the business known up until then as Eastman & Bowden, now be renamed Bowden & Company, Commission and Forwarding Agents, to become the sole property of Morgan Bowden of Wolflock, New Mexico.

Clint lighted a short cigar.

'Have I got the story right, Attorney?'

Baca-Brown appeared somehow ill and shrunken in that huge chair now.

'Everything was fair, square and legal,' he croaked. He was a man who could carve you up in a court of law, but this situation was something very different. He was a little old man and this was a very tall young man with a glitter in his eyes now that was causing him a chill.

'Would have been had my father been really dead, you mean? He was a prisoner of war for two years but nobody was ever notified of this.' Clint's voice cracked like a whip. 'After the war the US illegally took him away to help rebuild the south. It was two more years before he got home.' He leaned forward, shoulder muscles straining through his shirt. 'Do you want to take the story from there, Attorney?'

The little man glanced helplessly towards the door. He jumped inches when a hammer fist crashed down on his desk, causing his monogrammed, gold-plated writing-set to rattle. At that moment he was too scared to speak.

'All right then, I'll tell it to you!'

Clint sucked in a breath. Since coming to this place, he'd done a lot of thinking, asked a lot of questions, got a bunch of answers. The more he learned the closer he felt he was getting to understand things that had happened in the past, but he still needed to know more until he was sure. This man in front of him could supply some answers, if he chose.

'We'll start where war vet Henry Eastman eventually comes home from the wars to be with his son,' he ground on. 'He's aged a hundred years and there's something eating at him. As soon as he's strong enough, he leaves me in charge again and comes south here to visit with his old 'partner', expecting to find out just how rich they'd both become during and after the war years. You still with me, mister?'

The attorney was the color of old parchment by this. His visitor seemed to have him hypnotized.

'Alone and sick,' Clint continued, 'he sees the Commission House, huge and prosperous-looking. But it doesn't have his name on it, just Bowden's. He's confused, he can't figure. So what does he do next? Come on, attorney man, you are the story-teller. You tell Henry Eastman's son what he did then. Did he come see an attorney here by any chance? Sounds a reasonable thing to do.'

'I . . . I had to tell him the truth. . . .'

'Which was?'

Clint knew the truth by this, or at least a large part of it. His father had spoken little of his visit to Wolflock down in Chavez County over the years. But he needed further information and confirmation from this man, had to have it before he went any further.

Baca-Brown's eyes were saucers and a droplet of sweat coursed down his skinny attorney's nose.

'Bowden forced me do it, son.'

'Do what?'

'To institute legal proceedings to have your daddy declared dead after nothing was heard of him in two years after Shiloh. A . . . judge owed me a favor and Mr Bowden wasn't sparing any expense. The finding was duly made and the company's articles were redrawn classifying Mr Bowden as sole owner.'

Clint leaned back in his chair.

'So what happened when Dad confronted Bowden?'

'Son, this was all a long time ago. Why stir it all up now? Your father is dead, you say? I'm very sorry. But what can be gained by raising a fuss now?'

'What can be gained? Good question. Well, even though I guessed at least half the truth about how he'd been gypped by his former partner, I was tied down up north and couldn't do a damn thing about it. Besides, Dad made me promise I wouldn't. He was too beat up by the war and Ma being long gone to want any fuss. So, I stayed on, helping Dad make a go of a lousy double section of dirt that would never pay its way, and which he'd never leave on account he was by then obsessed with building it up and leaving me something. I know he never wanted me to do anything, and I'd never have known what had happened if he hadn't talked when he was out of his head and close to death.'

The attorney almost feared to ask, 'What . . . what did he say?'

Clint leaned forward, his face iron.

'He was delirious. He told me how as soon as he was taken prisoner in the East, Bowden moved to have him officially declared dead ... and must have bribed or cheated to have this done the way it was by the War Office. He also told me that his ex-partner and ex-friend was living in New Mexico, that he'd visited him and was told he was not worth one red cent and was shown the documents to prove it – by Bowden himself. So howcome you look scared but not surprised? I'll tell you why. Your name was mentioned. And when I get the chance to investigate fully what took place down here all those years ago, I reckon I'm going to find you were involved. Do you know what that could mean for a rich, high-living and crooked attorney?'

'I ... I'm sorry I don't know anything about what you are saying. ...' The man's voice gave out on him and a thick silence enveloped the room.

A wagon rolled by with a sharp crack of a whip and creak of leathers.

The brass ship's clock on the rosewood bookcase chimed the quarter hour, and Baca-Brown sounded as though his throat was choked by dust.

'What ... what are you going to do now you know, er ... Clint?'

Clint stood, emotion working his features, his breathing uneven. He did not reply because he did not know the answer himself, even though he felt he now had a tacit admission of guilt.

The purpose of the mission which had brought him half-way across the West had been to discover for himself whether the person he loved most had been cheated out of his rightful share of their joint commission business.

Indicators and information had led him to this plush office suite and Baca-Brown's manner strongly suggested that it could well have been here that the crooked legalese was employed 'officially' to deny Henry James Eastman, and his son, any further profits from their joint venture.

What his next move should be was unclear. But Bowden had plainly robbed his father and hurried him to his grave. Was there a court on earth or in heaven which would allow such a crime to go unpunished?

He left without another word, leaving Wolflock leading attorney slumped grayly behind the big desk, loathing himself, afraid. Baca-Brown thought briefly of warning the man who had made him rich, but knew he wouldn't. He'd already done more than he should for Bowden. Far too much, most likely.

All over town coathangers were clicking and taffetas and calicos felt the smoothing touch of hot irons, while paint, powder, perfume and pomade were applied recklessly as the sun went down, ushering in the night of the Summer Ball.

Even down in shabby Old Town, Sunday bests were being trotted out and dusted off for the big occasion, despite the fact that few of them would see the inside of the big old Spanish-style hall tonight, admission prices having been carefully geared to keep the riff-raff outside with their noses pressed against the windows.

The Summer Ball was the season's major social occasion and its operation was securely in the hands of the best people. Tonight the handsome and the successful, the powerful and influential and the Haves, as opposed to the Have Nots, would meet and mingle beneath bunting and

Chinese lanterns, would get to glide stylishly over freshly waxed floors and mingle mainly with others of their élite ilk.

This was Wolflock's opportunity to display its sophistication and the wife of a banker, rancher, importer, railroad tycoon or hot-shot entrepreneur would have to be at death's door from Yellow Jack fever before she would fail to sail through those big yellow-wood doors somewhere between half past eight and nine tonight.

The murmur from the street reached faintly into the fitting-room of the town's top tailor who had worked himself almost to a standstill that week. None the less, the man had enough energy left to compliment his last client as he stood back to admire the tailored jacket he'd just slipped over the man's shoulders.

'Ah, Señor Forte, so many have the finances but not the figure, while for so many others it is the opposite.' He was pocketing the fat wad of cash the tailored broadcloth suit had cost. 'But happily in your case the figure and the finances have met and married successfully tonight. *Madre*! The *señoritas* will surely fight over you. I, Miguel, predict it.'

Although vain as a peacock and normally sharply conscious of his appearance, swashbuckling Slim Forte appeared something less than impressed as he studied himself in the floor-to-ceiling mirrors. Immaculate suit, dazzling white shirt and black tie, crimson cummerbund and glossy patent-leather boots. But surely something was missing?

He snapped his fingers and turned to lift the handsome double gunrig and cartridge-belt off the back of a chair.

Miguel slapped his plump cheeks in horror as Forte

93

began buckling the twin sixshooters around slim hips.

'*Nombre de Dios* – *no, señor*! This is akin to cutting the finest wine with the beer.'

Too late. The guns were on. The tailor threw up both hands and poured himself a brandy. Forte remained unmoved.

'It's all right for you, Mig. Nobody wants to sneak up behind you in the middle of "The Pride of Erin" and let you have six in the kidneys, do they?'

The tailor's tired smile faded. He catered alike to the gentry and the rough trade, when it could afford him. Slim Forte fitted snugly into the rough-trade category despite the man's relentless efforts to climb the ladder of success and acceptance in this big river town.

Rumors abounded concerning Forte and the big money he threw around, and it was common knowledge that the man was setting his cap for Rachel Bowden, surely an indicator of blind ambition. Many whispered that the dashing gunman was an outlaw, a rustler, possibly even an escaper from Yuma. Miguel only knew him as a personable if volatile customer with a reputation for hurting people, occasionally even killing someone or other in a gunfight, usually in some other town. He scared this tailor, which proved that Miguel was an intelligent man. But he went on staring quizzically at the gunman for maybe a second or two too long, his doubts and uneasiness suddenly showing plain.

That was a mistake.

'Here, gimme that,' snapped Forte, taking the glass from his hand. 'And get the hell out, I've got some figurin' to do. Go on, vamoose!'

This was the tailor's own place yet he vacated quickly.

Slugging down the grape, Forte lowered his tailored back-side onto a table-edge and produced a silver cigar-case, purchased especially for the night ahead.

Tonight, in this quiet time before the action at the hall began, he reviewed the week just past, assessing its pros and cons.

Credit side: two successful rustling raids upon Spanish Ranch and certainly more of the same ahead for himself and the strong bunch he'd strung together now. His long-term plan was to go on continually doing whatever it took increasingly to damage and weaken Bowden, while at the same time strengthening his own position from the proceeds of the rustlings he was staging with ever-increasing daring and success.

The result, he foresaw, would see Bowden broken and a new king of commerce, influence and power take his place.

Slim Forte.

His eyes glittered balefully.

Bowden was the biggest game in town – in the whole damned county! But Forte was about to accelerate his campaign dramatically – and torching that rich man's business empire might not be too far ahead – if that was what it took to bring him to his knees at last.

He inhaled luxuriously.

He knew most would think it insane that any gunslinger-cum-thief-cum-whatever other murky enter-prises he might have in mind, should even aspire to semi-legitimacy in the everyday world.

But he'd seen former members of the Dark Brotherhood graduate to the respectable life, providing they came up with sufficient hard money to buy off both

the law and their enemies, and demonstrated the confidence and everyday plain guts to pull it off.

The way he saw himself in comparison with rivals on
either side of the law, was faster, meaner and smarter. But
mainly he was more ambitious and totally ruthless when
the chips were down.

Then the debit side reared its ugly head. There was a
new danger on the landscape. Clint. Suddenly that bastard
was pistol-whipping Cousin Jacks and acting like he was
someone important. And now, to rub salt into the wounds,
that Northerner had somehow wormed his way into the
good books with Rachel.

Clint – and just what breed laid claim to but one name
anyway – had also made him look bad for a second time in
the aftermath of the shoot-out at the mansion. Slim Forte
was strong and growing stronger every day, yet certainly
couldn't afford too many failures such as that farce at the
Bowden headquarters, he reasoned soberly.

Through others, Forte had recently whipped up the
growing mood of anti-Bowden sentiment as part of his
campaign to wear the Big Man down, weaken him, then
maybe force him into doing something crazy that might
serve to speed his way to the bottom, where Forte wanted
him.

Instead, the Coloradan had horned in and thrown all
his plans off course, and of a sudden folks were beginning
to talk. Not about Slim Forte, but rather one-name Clint.

Increasingly, he was growing deeply suspicious of that
tall hardnose. First up, he'd sized the man up as likely
dangerous in his way, but likely nothing to worry a man like
himself. Now he wasn't so sure. Just another wang-and-
rawhide drifter . . . or maybe something far more sinister?

Undercover lawman or cattle-company private dick, maybe?

He swore softly. He was in danger of letting events make him edgy. That simply wasn't the Forte style. He was the bandmaster, not the performing bear in this borderlands circus.

His lip curled as he ground the smoke out beneath a patent leather boot. Whatever the man was or wasn't, Clint was pushing it now. This was a war between Forte and Bowden, even if Bowden wasn't aware of it yet. The outlaw was not about to stand back idly and simply allow some crummy outsider to muddy the waters and maybe ruin his plans, that was for sure.

He left Miguel's side door swinging open and headed down the alley for the street. By the time he reached it, he was feeling good again, viewing every passer-by as an inferior and a loser. They were the meek. But they would not inherit the earth. He would.

Above the traffic sounds he could faintly hear the orchestra tuning up at the hall. Carriages laden with stylishly dressed folk wheeled by. He deliberately stepped in front of one, and the driver wasn't going to stop until Forte caught his eye. The rig stopped with a jerk, throwing people about inside. Forte flashed a big white grin at the driver and continued across the Avenue. Balls was what it was all about, and he had them.

There was one stop to make before heading on to the dance. Clancy's was an off-Main dive close by where the rough workmen from the Font tended to congregate. A place where such low-lifes could drink and gripe about poverty and long shifts and plan feeble rebellions against their bosses.

Doubtless the Jacks would have even more to bellyache about than usual right now in the wake of their ill-fated protest march upon North Hill. If the town might have a new hero tonight, then the Cousin Jacks had a new villain – the very man whom Rachel Bowden had accepted as her partner tonight.

He found O'Malley, Walker and Watts waiting for him in the smoky back room as scheduled. Walker and Watts showed the black-and-blue after-effects of last night's battering, but O'Malley was unscathed. The fat Irishman who bossed the Font's union was the typical leader type who preferred to send the men over the top while he observed well back from the front.

O'Malley started in apologizing for the failure of the march but Forte silenced him with an easy gesture. They'd followed the plan, he said magnanimously, hauling a fat roll from an inside pocket of his immaculate jacket. Clint's intrusion had been unforeseen, he conceded, but the overall objective had still been achieved. Bowden had, for the first time, been openly harassed on his own turf, winding up an unprecedentedly bad week for the so-called King of Wolflock.

Slim Forte rated this a plus and paid out accordingly.

None but these three knew that Forte was financially backing the miners' union's recent increased agitation. With his successful rustling operation taking a heavier and heavier toll on Bowden, the rebellious miners were providing the second prong to Forte's co-ordinated pincer attack upon Bowden's empire.

He'd observed how ruthless men with brains clawed their way to the top in other places, and he was employing whatever weapons were available to get there by climbing over Morgan Bowden's carcass.

The Jacks wanted to talk on but Slim was hungry to get amongst the élite who would soon be his social and commercial equals.

He was quickly on his way and was not to be diverted again until he spied the man Clint nursing a glass in a front window at the Long Rail. He pulled up sharply. The gunman fingered his cheek where a nerve began to twitch, then slowly mounted the steps onto the porch and stood watching the tall man toss down a swallow of rye like it was lemonade.

So howcome this new hero and Romeo was not off picking up his date?

He strolled right in. Clint gave him a flinty stare. They were men cut from similar cloth and simply bound to clash. It was in their genes. One was a flashy outlaw, the other a sober man of the land only recently released from the bondage of a hard-scrabble spread in the North. Yet there was a common factor; both were driven and dangerous.

'What are you looking at, sonny?' Clint challenged softly. He'd always played the game hard.

'Give it a name and you can have it, daddy.'

Clint drained his glass and got up, hitching at his belt. He too was dressed for the ball but was nowhere near as sartorially stylish as the other. But he was considerably taller and made sure Forte was aware of this as he loomed before him. The gunman smelt the liquor strong on his breath.

'How's the cattle business, Forte?'

Slim stared. 'What?'

Clint grinned. He was simply fishing. For reasons of his

own he was intensely interested in the recent rustlings, hence the high-risk time he'd spent hunting for sign in the Sweet Alices. He was half-way suspicious about Forte, who had a reputation and a certain maverick look. The man was also super-confident, always remarkably well-heeled, and seemed to give off the faint whiff of owl hoot.

'Relax, cowboy,' he drawled. 'You're acting kind of edgy.'

'Could be you're actin' foolish, big man. Like real foolish.'

Clint moved. Whether he was turning for the batwings or making to shove the other out of his path, was unclear. But suddenly Slim had a Colt in his fist. He rammed it into Clint's short ribs.

'You're drunk, Clint – or whatever your freaking name is. So back off before you get to be dead too. But where's Rache's taste? I can see now you're just another booze-hound bum. A nothing!'

Clint sobered as he backed up a pace. Forte was at least half-right; he had drunk too much. It had been a long, hard day.

'Get out!'

It was Forte's call and he held the cards. Clint just nodded and disappeared through the batwings.

You could hear the quiet.

# CHAPTER 7

# 'I ACCUSE!'

'You dance very well, *señor.*'

'And you, *señorita.*'

'And if it isn't too bold for me to say so, you are very handsome in your evening clothes.'

He searched for the right words needed to repay her compliment. They did not come easy. He was certainly in no way shy but simply had little experience with women from the high side of town. But if his tongue wasn't operating quite the way he might want it to, his eyes were functioning perfectly. He was surprised how easy it suddenly became to say, 'You're the finest-looking woman here tonight . . . by a country mile.'

Rachel Bowden smiled pleasurably and flicked a speck of dust from his shoulder in a proprietary way which Clint found entrancing. And they glided beneath the multicolored lights of the Chinese lanterns, slowing as they passed the official table in order that the Bowdens could see their niece and cousin. The brothers beamed proudly but

Bowden appeared preoccupied, seated there at the head of the brilliantly festooned table surrounded by hard-jawed and silver-haired fellow captains of commerce of his own powerful ilk.

The orchestra changed tempo. This was the signal for other men to get up and cut in if they so desired – and Clint felt a tap on the shoulder, a heavy tap.

'May I?'

Slim Forte was smiling confidently, as well he might, being by far the most impressive male in the music-filled hall.

'Oh, I'm so sorry, Slim, but I did promise Clint this full set of dances,' Rachel said. 'Didn't I?'

She had done no such thing. Yet Clint quickly nodded and managed a smile. 'Better luck next time . . . son.'

There was just one flicker – no more than a breathless moment – when something red and fathomless burned in Forte's blue eyes and danger breathed close. But quickly the look was gone and the man reached past Clint to chuck Rachel under the chin in a proprietary kind of way, then managed a smile that came straight off the peaks of the Sierras.

'Save me the Gordon, brown-eyes,' he said. 'That's always been our favorite, anyway.'

The couple continued on but neither was as relaxed as before.

'He's very angry because I accepted your invitation, Mr Clint.'

'Just call me Clint. All my friends do.'

She studied his features intently. 'Do you have many friends? I don't really know much about you, do I?'

A couple collided with them. It was Sheriff Watson and

Elspeth. Everyone laughingly apologized and Clint was almost relaxed again as they moved on.

'Not many,' he replied to her query. 'But then, not many enemies either.'

'But you do have some enemies?'

He murmured a vague response, the irony of her query weighing across his shoulders. For the only genuine enemy he had here was her uncle. But if that were the case, what was he doing gazing into her eyes and enjoying the brush of her supple body against him? Should he be playing up to the man he'd come to nail to the cross, if possible?

Everything he'd done here up until now had been planned and deliberate; getting a feel for the place and its people; seeking out the acquaintance of those who searched for rustler sign in the Sweet Alices; confronting Attorney Baca-Brown and sensing the man's guilt and fear. All had had their purpose and all were logical and part of his mission in the South . . . all but this woman in his arms.

His setting out to ingratiate himself with her uncle, the man whom he was now virtually certain had somehow bluffed and cheated his father out of what would rightly have been his own by now, had been something intuitive and impulsive, maybe foolish.

Yet he did not regret it and was relaxed again by the time the orchestra took a break and Rachel insisted she needed air.

The hall's flower-decorated rear balcony overlooked a small sunken garden and was spacious, cool and semi-private. There were several couples in sight, including Slim Forte and the daughter of an importer from upriver. Forte was laughing at something the girl said. It sounded almost genuine.

Clint leaned his back against the balustrade and gazed at the stars. For a short space it was still and he almost wished all this was really innocent and genuine; the man with the lovely woman, the placid border night, the soft breezes whispering up from the river.

Too bad it only appeared a perfect picture. And suddenly he was cursing himself for delaying his plans just for tonight, when he could have been many miles away pursuing the course which had brought him here.

But when he glanced at her and she smiled, something within betrayed him. He swallowed at the very way she looked, so vitally alive with raven hair stirring in the breeze.

'I wonder why, Clint. . . .'

'Huh?'

'Why you asked me . . . and why I accepted. . . ?'

The hell with talk! Suddenly she was in his arms and he crushed her against him, her lips setting him afire when she responded with reckless passion.

'Miss!'

They broke apart and whirled to face Morgan Bowden.

'Really, Uncle,' she chided. 'Are you spying on me?'

'You know better than that. Your cousins wish to see you . . . inside. They appear upset about something.'

'I can't imagine what,' Rachel retorted sharply. She swallowed, then turned to her escort with a sigh. 'Oh, all right. Please excuse me, Clint.'

'Surely.'

He stood back watching uncle and niece vanish indoors, then fired up a crooked brown Mexican cigarillo. Somehow the fragrance of the tobacco smoke seemed to blend perfectly with the velvet night. But he was in no way relaxed. Slowly his expression hardened and muscles rippled along the lean jawline. 'Right now, Clint,' said an inner voice, 'is the right time to go. Make any excuse, but go. Get the Sam Hill out of here!'

Horse sense warned that whatever was building up here in this Southern town, whatever outcome there might be for his quest for either justice or vengeance – he might even be a target himself now.

'You're going to need a clear head before you're through here, and there's no guarantee you'd have it with her around to cloud your thinking and fill your head with impossibilities,' he warned himself. 'Like her. . . .'

Bowden was at once both his perceived enemy and Rachel's relative-guardian. What future could there be in a situation like that? She would only be a diversion from what you've got to do, he told himself firmly, and almost believed it. Eventually the music struck up again and the balcony began to empty.

Deliberately he conjured up images of his father's last years compared with his former partner's position of wealth, power and luxury. And this time he had no trouble hardening himself simply by reviving in his mind the oath he had sworn over his father's grave.

The strains of a Stephen Foster melody welcomed him back into the hall. He needed a shot and was making for the bar at the front when, glancing across at the official table, he sighted a familiar face at the Bowden table, indeed seated at the big man's side, heads close together, animated.

It was Wolflock's premier attorney whom he'd been forced to visit and seek his advice.

Sight of the two together in deep conversation warned him that he'd almost certainly made an error of judgement, and that the attorney had obviously overcome his fear of him and decided to 'go with the strength' – Mr Big.

He would like to believe he might square accounts with the silver-haired son of a bitch later – but had more than that on his mind now. He caught a glimpse of Rachel's strained face as she searched the crowd for him anxiously. He reckoned he knew now why her uncle had summoned her back inside. Most likely by now, the whole Bowden table knew what his real name was; that he was not just a tough drifter but the son of a man from Morgan Bowden's past, who had come here bent on some kind of mischief or vengeance!

It was a taut moment, but quickly he calmed, forcing reason to take over from emotion.

So what if his secret was out? Had to happen sooner or later. Naturally, Rachel would not want anything to do with him now.

He would calmly finish his drink and simply disappear. Or might he have two? One for the road, and another for the heartache.

'Don't you drink too much, Ike Watson.'

'This is only my third, Elspeth.'

'Your third before supper, don't you mean?'

'Don't nag, woman.'

'Don't call me that!'

Ike Watson, barely recognizable in dinner-suit, boiled shirt and four-in-hand tie, glanced around to see people dancing their way. The lawman in him noted the presence of Slim Forte, Clint, and Bowden and his party. Then his date gave him a nudge and he turned back to her with a totally fake smile.

'Well, don't nag, Pretty Elspeth,' he chided gently.

She took his hands and they began to dance again. 'You're a difficult man, Ike Watson. Why is it you suspect everybody?'

'Huh?' he said, nonplussed. 'What are you talking about, woman?'

'There you go again!'

'Elspeth. What—'

'Don't worry, I saw your beady eye pick out Mr Bowden, Slim Forte and that gentleman with Rachel. You're suspicious and can't help wondering what they might all be up to, can you?'

The lawman sighed and concentrated on his palais glide. But she was right, of course. He felt that something volatile was building with that trio. He only hoped he was wrong.


The bar, which was set up in a spacious alcove off the ballroom, was well patronized by both the big spenders who could afford the inflated prices, and several whose shabby clothes and general awkwardness tabbed them as Have Nots who had pinched and scraped to give themselves just one night amongst the gentry.

He was mildly surprised to see Wash O'Malley, the miner's union boss, togged out in a half-way presentable outfit. The rugged workers' organizer was knocking back the hard stuff in the company of a hatchet-faced stranger with a shoulder-holster bulge showing plainly beneath his jacket.

Clint sank the first fast, lingered over the second and was almost through when a sudden crash sounded from the ballroom bringing the music to an abrupt halt.

It proved to be just an accident. A Mexican in shabby *charro*, with a little too much tequila on board, had lost his footing on the waxed floor and had fallen across an empty chair at the official table, upsetting some of the decorations.

But then an angry-faced Bowden was shouting orders, and Jim Kidd and several Company security men appeared from nowhere to seize the drunk. They began bundling him towards the side doors. The man objected and tried to dig in his heels. Bowden shouted again and Kidd socked the man in the jaw, sending him glassy-eyed with blood spilling from his gaping jaw.

Clint saw red.

'Hold up!' he shouted, shouldering his way through the circle of dancers. His emotions, so carefully locked away for so long, were beginning to seep out. It might have been the liquor, but suddenly he felt like the defender of the little man and the enemy of the rich and powerful.

Closing in on the group, he shoved one out of his way to confront Kidd. 'What the hell do you think you're doing, mister?'

'Er, followin' orders, Mr Clint.'

'Get them both out of here, Kidd!' Bowden shouted from the table. 'The derelict and that troublemaker both.'

'Touch him again and you'll answer to me,' Clint warned Kidd, who faltered under his cold stare.

He turned and approached the long main table which was groaning beneath the weight of glassware, bottles and food.

He halted.

'This is just your speed, isn't it, Bowden? Walk right over anyone who's not big enough or rich enough to strike back. You've made a career of it and people hate your guts for it, but are just too blamed scared of you to do anything about it. Just how long do you reckon you can get away with treating people like nothings? How long before this simple-minded town realizes it's been run by a crooked, thieving son of a bitch all these years, and decides some-one should do something about it?'

He paused.

The huge room was gripped by a congealing silence as Bowden stood with jaw agape, his men looking to him for guidance.

But Clint held the floor. 'You're not going to do anything, and I guess I can't blame you. Maybe you're happy to have someone walk all over you, which makes me different from you, I guess. . . .'

He made for the doors. Light-footed and fast, Slim Forte stepped in front him. 'Not so fast, scum. You're not leavin' until you apologize to Mr Bowden.'

'Get out of my way!'

Forte's hands rested on his gun handle. Suddenly every-one was rising and backing away from two tall men facing across ten feet of gleaming floorboards.

'No chance to get the jump on me a second time, pilgrim.' Forte smirked. 'Not goin' to turn my offer down too, are you? If you do, you're gonna have to apologize or I just might have to blast you whether you go for iron or not. The choice is up to you!'

'That will be enough, Forte,' called Sheriff Ike Watson, detaching himself from the ring of dancers packed around the walls. 'Just back up. There will be no violence here.'

'But—' Forte began, but Rachel cut him off as she came hurrying across the open space.

'Have a little sense, Slim,' she chided. 'Carrying on like this in a room filled with people!' She hooked her hand into the crook of Clint's right arm. 'Come along, Mr Clint, I'll see you out!'

'Rachel, come back here this instant!'

Bowden's shout went unheeded. Someone gave a hearty cheer of pure relief as the couple vanished through the throng in the vestibule. Moments later the orchestra launched into a spirited rendition of 'Turkey in the Straw'.


All Chavez County baked under a pitiless sun that day but the hottest place of all might well have been here at the bottom of this yellow-walled arroyo where the heat was trapped and concentrated with no place to go.

Clint's shirt was plastered to his back and his intent face gleamed with sweat as he knelt on one knee, delicately fingering the hoofprints in the dust.

Despite the brutal heat and the distress of his horse where it stood hipshot and head-hanging nearby, the man was a picture of calm concentration as the oppressive midday silences of the Sweet Alice Hills pressed down upon him. It was his third straight day in the hills, spent searching for sign, analyzing whatever he found, dismissing some, following up on others. He'd been out here several times before this blistering week of fiery weather came surging up from out of Mexico's stony deserts. But this was the first total effort he'd put into his own private manhunt. Once before, when plodding Sheriff Watson had surprised him scouring Buzzard Canyon to the south, he'd given the lawman a gratis tip on some middling suspicious tracks he had come across.

On that occasion he'd not had the time to pursue the sign further himself. Naturally Ike had not come up with anything. But right at this moment, Clint was focused on just one faint set of tracks made by a horse with an inward turning off-back hoof which was one of those he'd slotted away in his head earlier as worthy of closer investigation, should he encounter it again.

He had seen a set of prints like this not far from the nest of granite rocks where two Spanish Ranch riflemen had been shot to death a week earlier.

He uncoiled to his feet and followed the arroyo's westward course with eyes slitted narrowly against the shimmering glare.

Having already established that this sign existed only in this strip of sand and dust, fading away where the arroyo floor turned stony, his first task had been to convince himself that this was indeed the same fiddle-footed horse which had left its tracks at the murder site. Now this had been accomplished it was time to forget sign for the moment and have recourse to the far more inexact science of guesswork.

The arroyo forked into a dozen branches half a mile beyond the next bend; if he were a rustler with a hideout in the harsh hills, which of those branches might he follow?

Walking his horse, he climbed up the crumbling arroyo wall and covered a mile afoot to reach a low mesa. Here he tethered the horse and climbed alone to the crest which took a brutal half-hour and left him gasping like a grampus by the time he gained the summit.

Times like this he had cause to appreciate the endless years on the Windy Hills ranch where his father had dreamed and he had slogged like a slave trying to convert that dream into a reality. That he had failed in this objective was unarguable. But he had succeeded in acquiring a physical and mental toughness second to none. He needed all he could drum up of both to keep going out here, seeking to do alone what had thwarted many men over a long period of time.

Half an hour later he found himself studying the thin, dark stain of a waterfall which marked a bluestone cliff sloping down out of higher regions several miles westward. Following days of searching the hills this was the first sign of running summer water that he'd sighted. The hoof-prints he'd examined pointed in that general direction. This was guesswork at its most imprecise, he was telling himself as he half-walked, half-slid down the mesa face, but with nothing better in his locker he would follow it up.

It was a slow ride. You could kill a horse in this heat. He was fully alert as he moved through barricades of coarse vegetation and traced a track between outcroppings of stone, riven and carved into fantastic shapes by time and the elements, but his thoughts were elsewhere.

More than ever he knew his impulsive decision to attend the ball with Bowden's niece had been a mistake. Not because of his exposure as Henry Eastman's son; that had always been inevitable. It was his time with Rachel and what had happened at the ball that had pierced his armor and left him emotionally wounded as a result.

How bizarre that he should fall for the niece of the man he hated, how wildly unexpected that wealthy and sophisticated Rachel Bowden should seem to return his feelings.

In a sudden uncharacteristic moment on the ballroom balcony, he'd found himself confiding just about everything about himself and his history, apart from the reason that had brought him into her life. She was touched when he spoke of his father and he had seen unshed tears in her eyes during the telling, as indeed there may have been in his.

Clint had refused to reveal what he'd uncovered about their relatives' old partnership. If Bowden wanted her to know this he could tell her himself. He didn't want to hurt her any more than he must. At least not yet.

He was still as committed as ever to bringing Bowden down even though this would surely cost him infinitely more now than he could have foreseen before first laying eyes upon the man's niece. He would throw away any vestige of hope he might have had with Rachel; there was likely an even greater chance that he might lose his life into the bargain now.

The enemy was alerted, and he was not about to underestimate Morgan Bowden's ruthlessness for one moment.

The horse was played out as that Triassic sun sank behind the ridges, its last rays setting fire to the underbelly of a thunderhead that threatened rain to the north. But Clint was content to walk, sixgun in hand, as he made his way over a cedar-topped hill to drift down a long covered slope of solid green timber and healthy grass. Waterside country.

He inhaled the good green smells of the water, so welcome after the harshness of the hills, and propped sharply when he caught a whiff of what could only possibly be the aroma of stew simmering in a pot.

A short spell later saw him drop belly flat upon a grassy

ridge with an unlighted cigar between his lips, gazing down upon a comfortable campsite on the bank of the little waterfall creek where six or seven gunhung men were calmly preparing supper.

He started at a close sound and, craning his neck, realized there was a sentry leaning on a rifle in the brush not thirty feet below.

Clint drew his Colt and cocked it without realizing he'd bitten his cigar in half.

# CHAPTER 8

# DARK ALLIANCE

Morgan Bowden stared haggardly across the desk into the homely face of Ike Watson.

'All right, Sheriff, you win. I'll consider having you allocated your extra deputies. It's growing plainer by the day that you are incapable of maintaining the level of law and order we deserve and need. How many men do you want and when do you want them?'

Even when conceding a kind of defeat, Bowden couldn't help but strike out. The big man was well aware that one lawman could not be expected to cope with the worsening troubles Bowden had been encountering recently. Watson was simply one man struggling to do the work of four or five. The sheriff had lost ten pounds' weight over the past month trying to keep abreast of the lawlessness, particularly the rustling, which was now his major concern.

But Ike Watson wasn't griping, and during his past few weeks of eighteen-hour days had developed a flinty toughness he never knew he had, a change in him which was visible now as he stared Bowden in the eye.

'The time for extra help is long past,' he said soberly. 'Don't need it now, won't have it. I'm making progress on the rustling and I don't want to be trying to break in a bunch of rube deputies when I should be concentrating on the main game.'

'You're a fool!'

'And what are you, Mr Bowden? A man who attracts enemies like flies to a pot-roast because you walk all over people, won't pay them honest money, flaunt what you've got like a hairy miner coming down to the agency for his once-a-year blowout? Men wouldn't thieve off you, and they sure wouldn't get drunk and try to bust up your house, but for the way you treat them.' He paused, then added deliberately, 'And whatever you did to that Clint feller's old man way back when . . . why, I guess you should-n't have done that either.'

There was a shocked silence. The lawman had never been this outspoken before. Bowden was deeply offended both by the lawman's suddenly truculent air of righteous-ness, but even more so by his allusion to Clint.

'Just what do you know about that man from Colorado, Watson?' he said menacingly, getting to his feet. 'Has he been griping to you as he did to – well, never mind who. What the hell is he about? I demand to know.'

Ike Watson leaned back in his chair and linked hands across his weskit.

'Why don't you ask him – Mr Bowden?'

Bowden was white as he jammed on his big white Stetson hat. Nobody ever spoke to him this way, especially not plodding Ike Watson.

'How dare you! Your manner is insubordinate. This will be the end of you, Watson. I'll have that goddamn tin star

116

off you and see you back in the gutter where your breed belong! And you can whistle for your deputies now.'

'Well,' Ike drawled, opening a drawer to produce a fat, dog-eared file two inches thick, which he dropped onto the desk top. 'When you get a replacement I guess I'd better spend a couple of weeks with him bringing him up to date on this.'

'What is it?'

Watson rose, leafing through pages of handwriting and pasted-up press cuttings.

'Everything I've been able to assemble on every rustling and every known rustler operating along the border over the past year.' He tapped the file. 'And I'm narrowing it down. I've had peace officers from Tucson, Nogales, Douglas, Agua Prieta and right through Wilcox, Cochise and Bowie feeding me information and hunches. I've got names, records, those jugged and those acquitted.' He looked up. 'I'm not a good enough tracker to find these cattle-bandits in the wild country, don't have either the time or the manpower for that. But sooner or later something's going to click, and I'll land you your thieves, with any luck, before you get the council to fire me.'

He meant every word. Bowden could tell. Watson was a plodder but a smart and relentless one. If he claimed to be making progress with the rustlings that were causing him so much harassment, Bowden knew it was the truth. Up until recently, when the incidence of cattle-thieving from Spanish Ranch had increased dramatically, Bowden had been prepared to accept the raids as a nuisance rather than a major problem. Not any more. The raids were increasing, while the miners' agitation was ongoing and eating into his production. He'd long considered himself

117

too big to be seriously damaged or hurt, yet he was hurting now.

And now the Clint business.

Attorney Baca-Brown had predictably passed on details of Clint's visits to him, and Bowden had been edgy ever since. Everything relating to his former business partner, Henry Eastman, had been thought safely buried in the distant past. He'd regarded himself totally in the clear and secure in that regard, but alarm had reared its head and sent a shiver of uncertainty through him at the merest hint that those long-ago matters might possibly be revived.

He had people investigating this Clint's background up in Colorado, without success. But he knew in his own mind that should that man's activities offer any genuine threat, then he would know exactly what was to be done with him.

He'd already barred him from his house, despite his niece's protests. He'd had men attempting to follow his movements but the man from Colorado kept proving too slick and smart for them.

He threw a brandy down and waited for the liquor to do its soothing work. The old commission house business in Colorado was lost in the past by now, he mused, along with his former partner, Henry Eastman. This troublemaker would be quickly assigned to history also, if needs be.

He shook his head. Rebellious miners, rustling reaching plague proportions, now echoes of his far past threatening. Suddenly he felt besieged on his own turf, and that was not a situation he would tolerate.

In his mind he was shifting onto a war footing. He was rich and powerful with influential connections, could assemble as many loyal and lethal foot soldiers as money could buy, if needs be.

He was ready to concede that opposition and adversity had suddenly hugely snowballed and had caught him off guard, and maybe he'd been been guilty of having been too busy simply enjoying the fruits of his success.

Not any longer!

'The hell with everything!' he said petulantly, going to the door. 'But you just watch your step, Watson,' he barked, clamping hat to head. 'There's only one man in this town who's indispensable, and you're not him!'

With that he stamped from the law office, bristling with bad-tempered bombast as he crossed the gallery and headed for his waiting carriage.

Four heavily armed riders formed an escort around the carriage as it rolled off along the avenue, and suddenly Morgan Bowden realized that he was beginning to look almost like a prisoner in the town he virtually owned.

Watching the entourage recede, Ike Watson marveled at the fact that he'd had the gumption to speak up the way he had done. But the brief moment of satisfaction faded as he surveyed the street. Wolflock was unnaturally subdued, had been for days. The rustlings were continuing, there were ongoing breakouts of violence between miners and towners and it seemed to Ike Watson that under the silence an erratic and menacing pulsebeat had begun to throb.

Two horsemen rode by. Strangers. Hard bitten riders with the wolf look about them. Rustlers? Who would know?

With a sigh he collected his hat and headed off for the telegraph office. Right now, he was working a different angle. He was attempting to find out from contacts in other places where the Spanish Ranch rustlers were unloading their stolen beef, a process which he reckoned had a far better prospect of success than his attempting to play Kit Carson and flush that gang out of their Sweet Alice labyrinths.

Passers by on the plankwalk shot their sheriff sympathetic looks as he tramped by. Nobody envied Ike Watson his job these days.

The tall figure walked the darkening streets alone. There was a chill in the air tonight that reminded him of home – and home would always be a patch of fair-to-rough cattle country up in Colorado.

A drunk swayed by, accidentally brushing his shoulder. Clint growled at the man but he continued on his way, oblivious. 'Drunk and likely to get even drunker,' he muttered. Then he thought treacherously, 'But it just could be that even he is smarter than you, Eastman. . . .'

He halted to roll a smoke. 'Might as well face it, mister; you're running out of options in this man's turn. You made a splash early on, but for days now . . . nothing. You can't get to see her – Bowden won't allow it. You put your cards on the table with Baca-Brown . . . and you're good as certain he handed the lot to Bowden on a platter. You've been snooping and fishing and finding out nothing, so. . . .'

He broke off at a different thought. 'That other attorney . . . you decided he wasn't up to the job, so you just forgot about him! Mebbe. . . .'

Shotgun Alley seemed darker and crummier even than before. A shadowy urchin tried to touch him for a dime and he sent him scooting with a curse.

The crummy office at the end of the alley was wrapped in darkness. He climbed the steps and hammered on the rickety door beneath the barely legible Burge Burge Clackett & Burge sign.

No response.

'Who ya lookin' for?'

The urchin was back.

'Who do you think. . . ?' he began, then broke off. He fished in his pocket for a coin. 'Where is Clackett, kid?'

'Gorn.'

'I figured that. Gone where?'

'Dunno . . . but I can tell you a lie if you want?'

The kid was hazing him – the whole town seemed to have ganged up on Clint Eastman. He started off with a curse, paused, turned and flipped the coin back at the ragged figure who snatched it out of the darkened air and vanished.

The mood was riding him hard as he made his way along the plankwalks of the main street, giving way to nobody. He sensed what was building in his mind but tried to resist it, knowing how dangerous it was . . . reckless, if he was honest with himself. But he was growing desperate on this suddenly chill evening in Wolflock. Could be desperation called for desperate decisions?

He halted before the jailhouse. A drunk sang tunelessly from a back cell. He was about to move on when he glimpsed the lawman standing at his pot-belly fixing coffee.

Ike Watson showed no surprise when he entered.

'Howdy,' he drawled, returning to his desk chair. He took a sip. 'So . . . who have we been aggravating tonight?'

'Any coffee left in that pot?'

'Take a look and find out.'

He liked this badgeman. Almost everyone he'd encountered in this man's town seemed to be scared, devious, drunken or crooked in some way, but every instinct told him Watson was straight as a gunbarrel.

He poured a mug of joe and leaned a shoulder against the wall. Watson appeared old and tired and, with just a little encouragement from his visitor, admitted he felt like he was riding a losing streak so far as the recent brawling, shootings, rustlings and general combative character of his town were concerned.

Clint nodded as though understanding. He did. Watson was a good man who felt powerless to deal with the forces ranked against him.

That word 'powerless' brought him up sharply, and with sudden clarity he realized he'd allowed himself to begin drifting in that direction himself.

He straightened, jaw muscles working as he looked back.

His solitary life on the spread with his father away and the country filled with deserting soldiers from both sides, with marauding Indians, cattle-thieves and gangs of simple outlaws a constant threat to a lone kid on a section block, had, in retrospect, been a brutal proving-ground, a man-maker if ever there was one.

He'd killed his first would-be rustler when he was just sixteen. Over the lonely years ahead he'd defended the spread, hunted badmen before they got him, had lost count of the men he'd cut down, fulfilling his vow to keep the place intact for his father when he returned from the wars.

Slowly, he realized why his thinking was taking him in

that direction. He'd allowed himself to lapse in his purpose here, but now resolution was surging through him and he suddenly knew what he would do and how he would go about it.

Dangerous? For sure. Futile? Most likely. But considering the number of times he had tracked rustlers, fought rustlers and shot it out with that feral breed in the past, there had to be a chance.

He would do it. He would do it now.

'Where are you going?' the sheriff growled as Clint set his pannikin down and headed for the door.

But Clint Eastman was already gone.


Forte rode easy in the saddle, his barrel-chested gray moving smoothly beneath him. Ahead lay the hills, in back of him Lockjaw, which he'd just visited.

A standard freight locomotive hauling a string of heavily laden cars whistled stridently as it clanked out of the one-horser, making south for Wolflock. Likely laden with goods destined for Bowden's commission and forwarding company to make him even richer than ever, the outlaw speculated.

Night and day, winter and summer, trains, wagons, pushcarts and river barges brought an endless stream of produce to the doors of the Commission House where they were paid for, processed, then dispatched along every goat-track, back-trail, main highway and railroad track to be sold on at a fat profit by Morgan Bowden.

It had been on a day just like this almost a year ago now when Slim Forte, ragged, worn thin, and on the run from Mexican law, first stood by the railroad tracks in Wolflock and watched Bowden employees loading and unloading great piles of goods, and realized in a blinding flash that for twenty-seven years he had been a fool.

Gunfighting, rustling stock, chasing women, dodging the John Laws and blowing every cent he had on gambling and wild women. That had been Slim Forte, and it had been good. Your name on the front page, hard men giving way to you on the street, naming your own price to duel some loser who had it coming anyway.

But the negative side soon became all too plain. Nothing solid, going noplace, no real class or status. He was just a gunshark with style and he suddenly realized how badly he wanted to be something else. Something bigger. Bowden big.

He grinned broadly as the gray carried him swiftly away from the lines into the fastnesses of the hills. It was ironical that Bowden should be the man to inspire him and caused him to change both his thinking and his ways. Ironical, because once he'd seen Bowden and the plush commercial gold-mine the man had set-up here in Wolflock, he had determined to become another Bowden himself. Only bigger.

Bring the man down. Take what he had. Take every mother-loving risk in the book if that was what it took to achieve his ends. He was strengthened every day in his thrusting ambition by the powerful self-belief that had always been part of his make-up.

Slim Forte had what it took to succeed, so he had known passionately exactly what he wanted and hadn't hesitated to walk all over everybody to get it. Sure, maybe he'd done most of it semi-legally. So what? What counted was the goal. The ends justified the means. If he had a credo, that was it, and it was paying out in a big way right now, would eventually reap out in solid gold when Bowden was gone and he had replaced him as The Man.

Thrusting a hand into his pants pocket he hauled out a roll of bills fat enough to choke a steer. From far in the distance behind came the tinny shriek of the loco whistle. Ahead in the sky the tiny speck of an eagle circled high above the massive ruggedness of Frightful Mountain. This was a moment for the outlaw to know it was all coming together, when all those long months of observing, planning, recruiting, sheer hard work and risking his life on an almost daily basis were at last paying off.

He had a tough bunch of riders striking at some part of Bowden's empire every few days now. He had markets for his stolen stock; had Bowden hitting the whiskey hard – or so he'd heard.

He believed Bowden was slowly coming apart as he stepped up the raids while O'Malley kept the trouble-pot boiling out at the Font mine. Bowden was forced to sign on additional security every week now as Spanish Ranch continued to bleed. But by now Forte believed his gun bunch to be too big and well-organized for either Spanish Ranch cowhands or Sheriff Plod to deal with. His hideout was secure, his run-out route for the stolen stuff was operating with the efficiency of a railroad timetable. He could see no solid reason for him not to believe that final success was only a matter of time.

He rode on, watchful as always, but dreaming just a little now.

Even though the hideout was but an hour's ride into the hills from Wolflock, so naturally well concealed was it out along Pemmican Creek, behind miles of seemingly impenetrable cliff, canyon and thornbrush, that none of the many searchers who'd ventured into the Sweet Alices rustler-hunting had come anywhere close.

Nevertheless Forte's approach along the narrow twisting trail was wary as always. Caution and prudence were qualities he'd forced himself to acquire in recent times since setting his sights so high. Occasionally he could give way to his old gunslick's wild-headedness, but never out here, where it counted most. In the hills, or running fat cattle off Spanish Ranch by the light of the moon, he was invariably as cool and level-headed as any man making for the very top must be.

And yet his complacency took a huge jolt when, upon closing in on the creek, silent and careful as was his habit, the first thing he glimpsed through the trees was an unfamiliar red horse tied up to a tree.

The dazzling speed with which Forte hit ground with a cocked Colt in either fist spoke far more of gunfighter than rustler boss. He didn't seem to breathe as he cat-footed through thinning trees towards the natural clearing at the cliff base, but the alarm bells were stilled somewhat when he picked up the calm murmur of voices, and eventually glimpsed Doolin casually approaching the camp-fire clutching a steaming coffee-pot.

The red horse came into view again. Forte halted. The animal didn't belong to the bunch, and he recognized it now.

His scalp pulled tight. He didn't believe it. Clint?

He was a man ready to kill as he dropped into a low crouch and went forward at the run. Abruptly the trees gave way and there before him were Titus Poole and the boys standing around sucking back coffee and talking to the tall man with his back turned towards him.

Standing rigid in dappled sunlight, Slim Forte cocked both guns, causing everyone to swing about at the sound, Clint noticeably quicker than anyone.

'Reach, dead man!' Forte hissed.

'You?'

It struck the killer that Clint was as shocked to see him here as he was to see Clint.

An hour later and Clint was still talking.

Forte still had a naked Colt in his right hand but the weapon was now held angled down at the rocky apron before the caves as he chawed his way through a chunk of cold steak. It could be bleak and lonesome out here at times for the cattle-rustlers, but they ate well. Steak, mostly.

Clint was lucky to be alive, and knew it.

When he'd tracked down the camp in just a few hours, and took the rustlers' look-out into camp on the end of his gun, he'd been able to convince a startled Titus Poole and his henchmen that they should hear him out. He insisted he had no intention of handing them over to the law, claimed that they would soon understand that he had come with the exact opposite objective in mind, if they would just give him a hearing. When asked how he'd apparently scented out the hideout when armies of posses and cowboys had failed, he just shrugged. His violent and solitary upbringing in Colorado had made him the finest tracker in the county long before he was twenty. Scenting out the rustlers here had taken him longer than anything he'd tackled before, but he'd done it, would have been amazed had it been otherwise.

He'd been one against ten when he rode in. And when

he riskily housed his .45 and folded his arms to convince the cow thieves he was playing a straight game, Poole had decided he'd earned the right at least to be heard.

He wanted to join them, he'd insisted. That was his claim, and he seemed genuine. He had even come equipped with a reason that even these hellers could accept. Speculation concerning an alleged and long-forgotten shakedown by Morgan Bowden of his original business partner in his pre-Wolflock days, which had leaked out somehow following Clint's confrontation with Attorney Baca-Brown, had reached the rustlers' ears. He told the dangerous circle of outlaws that he meant to square accounts with Bowden, and spoke with such fierce conviction that they started to believe he spoke the truth.

Titus Poole had heard him out then discussed with him the possibility of some kind of merger, in a general way. At that time, Clint had no way of knowing that this black-bearded heller man was simply playing him along, waiting for Forte to show up through the tall timber.

Which he'd finally done, silently and glitter-eyed with a brace of cocked Colts.

'What the frag is going on here?'

The gang boss's face was tight with fury. Clint turned and gave him an easy grin. The Colts lifted fractionally. 'It's OK,' Clint said. 'I can explain. . . .'

'Then do it and be damn quick,' Forte snapped, stepping closer. 'If I don't like what I hear, you're a goner, pilgrim!'

Clint talked fast. Explained how he wanted to join the bunch to play a part in Bowden's downfall. He hinted at past grievances against the man, related how his attempts to get something on his man in Wolflock had failed, then his decision to seek out the one outfit that was hurting Bowden most, hoping to link up with them and pool their talents.

He was hammering what he considered to be his best selling points to a man whose handsome face was as expressionless as a Buddha.

He was a top trailsman and tracker, he insisted. Hadn't he just proved that by flushing the rustlers' hideaway when all previous attempts had failed?

He was tough enough to handle any situation; Forte already knew this from first-hand experience.

Then to his motive. He told them Bowden had ruined his father's life and he'd finally realized that he needed help to bring him to his knees. Revenge was his game. Claimed he didn't care a rap about profit, just so long as the books were balanced. Wouldn't Slim Forte want to get square with Henry James Eastman's cheating business partner, Bowden? Wouldn't anybody?

Forte suddenly broke in. 'Gimme a look at your hands.'

Clint obliged. Forte read the story of the callouses, then shot a questioning glance at Titus Poole, standing tall and rattlesnake lean at his side. Poole scratched his black-stubbled jaws and grimaced.

'Never seed a lawman or a badman with mitts like that, Slim.'

'That's because I've never been either,' Clint snapped, encouraged to speak out more forcibly now that he sensed Forte could be wavering. 'All my life, until now, I was too busy keeping my father alive working the meanest quarter section of dirt in Colorado Territory.'

He exhaled pent-up breath and rested hands on hips. His Colt now jutted from Poole's belt. They were allowing him to talk but weren't taking any chances.

'When I got here first, I was already sure about what had happened, knew I'd have to pay Bowden back or never look myself in the face again. I didn't know how I'd go about it until I realized he was up to his neck in trouble both with the miners and with losing cattle. Right away I got the notion of joining the opposition. I didn't fancy throwing in my lot with a bunch of blockhead Cousin Jacks . . . so I started looking for you boys. My showdown with Baca-Brown fired me up, I guess, and when I quit town last time I had made up my mind to ferret you out or die trying.'

He paused, stared hard at Forte, nodded.

'I'd be the most valuable man in your bunch, and I reckon you know it.'

Forte studied him a long silent time before rising. He shrugged powerful shoulders.

'You're right. I can't doubt you've got what it takes. And you might as well know I'm about to step up the raids double or treble right about now. There's going to be plenty of work and we'll have danger comin' out our ears . . . and I could sure use a top hand. . . .' He scowled. 'But how do I know I can trust you?'

'You don't.'

Somehow that seemed to be the right answer for, after a moment, Forte slipped his gun away and turned to his men. 'All right, I mean to give him a trial, but I want every geezer to watch him close. If anyone sees him actin' anyway he oughtn't, shoot him and tell me about it later.' He swung to Clint. 'Fair enough?'

'Sure. You won't regret it.'

Forte waved his men away, then approached.

'Get one thing straight. I mean to bring Bowden down then take over. What you get out of this is revenge, but not the spoils.' He tapped Clint's chest. 'That includes Rachel, savvy? I aim to bust her old uncle down to nothin' then move in with the money I'm makin' hand over fist selling his beef, and buy him out. Then I'm wedding Rache and we're gonna be the snootiest, richest couple in the county. You got that real clear, hero?'

'Yeah, I've got it.'

The outlaw's smile flashed white.

'Then why look so goddamn gloomy? Shake!'

# CHAPTER 9

# PAYBACK TIME!

The weeks that followed were the strangest and likely the most dangerous of Clint's life.

He was rarely out of the saddle, sometimes just with Forte, at others with the entire bunch. His time was spent reconnoitring Spanish Ranch, selecting vulnerable herds, noting the numbers and deployment of the cowboys – then striking.

The raids were hair-raising and harrowing for a man who had never stolen a dime in his life.

But once his desperate decision had been made, it was almost easy. You simply made the decision as to when, where and how you would strike, put your conscience and your fears in your hip pocket, made doubly sure your guns were loaded, then began praying.

But Forte lessened the risks greatly. It didn't take Clint long to recognize the fact that this man who was so skilled with the sixguns was even more talented when it came to thieving cows on the grand scale.

The pack-leader was obsessive about careful prepara-tion, but once his mind was made up and his plans completed it seemed the man relied heavily on instinct and daring to see him through. It was as though he sensed where and when the nighthawks might be either under-manned or careless – which of several run-out trails was better on the night. He knew when to run, when to make a stand. He even demonstrated on several occasions that he also knew when to cancel the most carefully scheduled plan if his sixth sense began acting up warning him some-thing didn't sit exactly right.

The band staged raids every third or fourth night.

As a result, life grew frantic on Spanish Ranch with Bowden continually adding to his gun strength while just as many of his men quit for the very sound reason that he was paying them ranch-hand wages while calling upon them to risk their lives doing the work of gunmen or lawmen.

With Forte money fuelling them, O'Malley and his miners in town kept the trouble-pot boiling out at Font mine, ensuring that neither Bowden nor his men could concentrate exclusively on the rustlings. In the early days it had taken Forte and the gang a whole month to blaze a secret trail to take them swiftly through the desolate Sweet Alices to Squaw Basin, and many was the night Clint found himself galloping through wind-gouged canyons and ford-ing fast-running creeks behind fifty or a hundred wild eyed cattle, with always the risk of a squad of angry cowboys riding in his dust.

Squaw Basin was a serene and peaceful spot, consider-ing its function. It was here that middleman Reece

Hatchette had set up his own organization to cope with the regular, small-time rustling which had prevailed in the region before Slim Forte came to town.

The crooked dealer had connections across the Mexican border at Agua Prieta, where he could command top dollar for prime American beef, and when mutual greed brought him and Forte together, both had proceeded to get rich hand over fist.

Forte ran the risk of getting caught and having his neck stretched in Wolflock while Hatchette's drovers chanced the border guards' guns while herding the stolen stuff into Mexico. Hatchette's risk? He liked to complain that he would likely die of boredom waiting here in remote Squaw Basin for Slim to come highballing down out of the pass behind another passel of prime cows. In other words, the risk for him was almost invisible.

Clint found he enjoyed spending two-thirds of his time riding a razor's edge of danger and the remainder crashed out from exhaustion. That way there was little opportunity to reflect too much on what he was doing. When such moments did arise and he might be pricked by an uneasy conscience, all he had to do was compare both his and his father's hardship lives in Colorado with the power, luxury and affluence of Bowden's existence to know that even if what he was doing was not right then it had to be just.

He even adjusted to the irony in a situation which saw him riding shoulder to shoulder with the one man from Wolflock, apart from Bowden himself, whom he disliked most. This sense of irony was compounded by the fact that he and Forte worked together like the parts of a Swiss watch. They synchronized so well, in fact, that they were pulling off the raids now without giving anyone the chance of even taking a shot at them. The risk of having to shoot some innocent cowboy was one very real possibility which Clint simply refused to face. He knew he could never kill an innocent man. So he threw everything into making the raids work smoothly and successfully in order that that prospect would simply not arise, and it didn't.

It was a strange feeling to ride into Wolflock during a rest period for the bunch, trotting past the Commission House, the rail depot, the Bowden bank and the Bowden mansion, then clatter right on by the jailhouse to reach the Long Rail, without drawing a suspicious glance from anybody.

Over a period of time the whole gang might visit the town in ones or twos. They needed the relaxation and, besides, even though citizens might look upon some of the rougher-looking hellions amongst them with some unease, there was no evidence to suggest that these hardcases were involved with the crime wave that was slowly but surely bleeding Bowden white.

On this day early in the fourth week since his Sweet Alice meeting with Forte, Clint reached town quietly in late afternoon, clean-shaven, neatly dressed yet drawn and slumped with weariness.

At ten the previous night the bunch had first diverted the nightriders on Spanish Ranch's remote north range with a grass fire, then run off some sixty head which were stampeded all the way through the hills to Squaw Basin by mid-morning. Although not scheduled to visit town today, Clint had insisted and Forte had wisely not stood in his way.

He knew why he was here, and it was not just to down a few stiff ones at the Long Rail.

It gave him a strange feeling to encounter Sheriff Watson as he quit the saloon later on his way to visit Rachel at the Commission House.

He liked the badgeman, sympathized with him because of the difficulties of his job, while at the same moment being responsible for many of those difficulties.

It was only as he stood on the corner talking with the man that Clint was forced to admit to himself he really felt almost like a genuine outlaw. Until that moment the name he'd labelled himself with was 'avenger.' But Watson's honest face was like a mirror in which reality was revealed. He was a crook, a stealer of other men's cattle.

Yet the inner voice which had driven him so powerfully ever since the death of his father and his decision to come south, again came to his aid; it isn't theft to rob a thief.

It might be flawed philosophy but it proved enough to strengthen him again.

Nor did he weaken upon approaching the Commission House which was scheduled to burn down very shortly – according to Forte.

Forte had convinced him that, while the Font troubles and the rustling were surely succeeding in dragging Bowden down almost to a vulnerable level, the Commission House remained the visible symbol of the man's power and wealth, and therefore it must go. After that was accomplished, Forte intended applying direct pressure on Bowden to sell out.

Clint believed that when this happened, he would feel that his vengeance was complete and he would be free to quit the owl hoot, as Forte seemed to sense he was desperate to do now.

That was his real goal now, he knew. To quit what he was doing. He'd played a major role in undermining the foundations of Bowden's empire, but every day it was growing that much harder. Living with scum, partners with a killer, forced to drain half a fifth of whiskey to sleep each night. There had to be a limit to how long an honest man could keep that up.

How smart he was to come to see Rachel in the North Hill mansion.

She'd bribed house hands to admit him secretly to her quarters, which luckily were semi-detached from the main house.

He'd recklessly visited her several times under these circumstances . . . risking his neck, maybe. But it was worth it. She kept him sane when he sensed he might be running on the edge of insanity – a clean-living, straight-shooting cattle rancher living the violent life of a rustler.

That was his thinking as the girl saw him off from the mansion at around ten that night. He had known instinctively that he needed this contact with normalcy and decency to give him the strength it would take to see out the final days.

Of course it was bizarre to walk, talk, dance and dine with the niece of the man he was committed to destroying, but then he'd always known the price would be high.

On one nocturnal visit he actually sighted Bowden in the gardens with his bodyguards, and was amazed at how the big man had deteriorated. His face red from drinking, his step unsteady, he'd appeared, to Clint's satisfaction, very much like a man coming apart at the seams.

By this time the unproven story of the early partnership

between Bowden and Henry James Eastman of Colorado had become general knowledge. It was believed by some, ridiculed by others. But it was also ancient history as far as most were concerned. But because it had painted Bowden in such a dismal light, the tycoon was at pains to convince his niece that Clint's allegations against him were false and malicious.

Rachel would have none of this, and said so. Unaware of Clint's secret life now, she was quick to defend him, pointing out spiritedly that if anyone should be offended and outraged, it should be Clint, having missed out on all the advantages he would have enjoyed had his father not lost his share of the early commission partnership, as he had done.

She was amazingly strong. And when supported to a careful degree by both her cousins, she proved at times strong enough to force her uncle to knuckle under when drink, anxiety and bitterness saw him attack the man she now believed she loved.

It was on this visit that they touched on the subject of the old partnership, and Clint was surprised and heartened by how strongly she spoke out against such things as deceit, unlawfulness and greed.

She would have been happy for herself and the boys to have simply shared their wealth. Such things were not important to her; she placed such things as integrity, honesty and a meaningful life far above them.

And hearing this, Clint wondered for the thousandth time – might he be paying too high a price for revenge? What if he were to lose her through all of this?

They embraced fiercely before he left and he had to fight not to tell her he loved her. And standing in flooding moonlight in the garden where he'd routed the miners, he had never been more aware of the double irony of the past weeks: partners with a man he detested, most likely in love with the niece of the man he must bring to ruin.

Yet just her words and touch somehow seemed to make everything magically right, at least for the time being. Heading for Main Street *en route* to the wild hills, he felt truly relaxed for the first time in many days, trying to figure how best he might salvage Rachel Bowden from the wreckage of what was to come.

He didn't glance at the stand of cottonwoods he passed a short distance from the mansion. There was no need. But had he done so he might have sensed movement there in black moonshadows as Slim Forte clamped white teeth around an unlit cigar.

'Friday,' announced Slim as casually as though ordering breakfast. Spooning sorghum into his coffee he looked up at the early sunlight shimmering through the spindly willows lining the burbling wild creek. His men stood in a wide circle all around him and every man jack of them looked up sharply from his Sweet Alice Hills breakfast of steak and potatoes on this young morning.

'Friday, Slim?' Titus Poole, nursing a slinged arm as a result of a nighthawk's lucky shot three days earlier, stood tall by the camp-fire. 'You mean—?'

'I mean, we're gonna do some burning, boy,' Forte smiled, cooling his joe with his breath. His startling blue eyes cut across to Clint where he stood brushing the red horse. 'It's time.'

'Thought we were going to make a try for that big herd

139

Bowden's got grazing out along the North Forty?' Clint remarked.

'I've decided different.' Forte's voice cracked with outdoor authority. 'I was walking and thinking on it last night and I realize we've done enough softening-up work now. We've been ridin' a winnin' streak ever since you joined us, Bowden's as good as run out of ideas on how to stop us, so the time has got to be ripe. So come all gather around, folks, and we'll hone up the details on how to do it. All going well, Bowden will be down six hundred head, his miners will be striking yet again, and his company palace will be a pile of ashes. Come Monday he will begging to sell up and get the hell out of town and that's when he'll find he's in real trouble. He'll find I'm the only buyer.'

He laughed boyishly, brimming with ruthless self-assurance and youthful vigor.

He fooled everybody but the wily Poole with his lightheartedness, but the tall rustler was forced to wait until after the hour-long discussion was at an end before getting the chance to to speak to him alone.

Titus Poole always talked straight. 'What's touched this off, Slim? You told me it wouldn't be until next week.'

Forte's face was as hard as something stamped from steel.

'Things change. I'm through waiting. We do it Friday and we're goin' to do it so neat that it'll only cost us one man.'

Poole stared. 'One? I don't figure?'

Slim jerked his chin in the direction of Clint, shaving with a cut-throat razor over by the creek.

'They're goin' to find that pilgrim at the scene of the

crime and he's gonna take the rap.'

'Clint? But I thought you and him was, you know, OK?'

'Don't think, *amigo*,' Slim Forte warned with a cold eye. 'Just leave that to me.'

He didn't mention Rachel or what he'd seen in town. But he was certain Clint was setting them up for a double-cross . . . should he get to live that long.


'Honestly, Ike Watson, sometimes I wonder about you, I really do. Here it is Friday afternoon and you have a thousand things to do before you escort me out to visit with Aunty Felicity tonight, yet I find you half-asleep behind your desk, wearing your worst shirt – and you haven't even shaved today. Are you deteriorating? If so, I rather think I should know in order that I might review my plans for the future, if you get my meaning?'

He could hardly fail. Elspeth was warning him to lift his game or they were through. She handed him an ultimatum like this every so often to keep him on his toes. Elspeth lived with the dread that one day he might just slide away into apathy and ineffectiveness leaving her looking very foolish for having ever entertained him as a possible suitor.

Ike looked a slob and knew it. What she didn't know, however, was that he hadn't been to bed in three days as law and order, both in Wolflock and out on the range-lands, crumbled all about him. He'd burned the midnight oil looking to re-establish peace out at the Font, ridden himself into the ground searching for rustlers, was growing accustomed to having citizens starting to treat him as a failure. Now Morgan Bowden was leading a Council push to have him fired.

Tired? He wasn't tired, just felt forty years of age going on ninety. And Miss Primly Perfect here expected him to shape up or else. Was this really who he wanted for a lawman's wife? he asked himself, and the answer came quick as a flash. You bet he did.

So he rose, patted down his hair, somehow forced a smile.

'Sorry, Elspeth, you're quite right, of course. I needed a dressing-down. Don't worry, I'll be on time, and neat.' His smile began to fade. 'Your aunt's influenza hasn't affected her speaking voice any, I hope?'

'Not at all, I'm happy to say. Why do you ask?'

'Heck, no reason,' he said. But inwardly he groaned. Elspeth's maiden aunt could talk faster than a Tennessee auctioneer. Just what he needed! Two or three hours of brain-damaging gossip, when about all that would do him one lick of good was about twenty hours' sleep or a break-through on the rustling.

When the woman left with a swish of taffeta and a waft of perfume, the sheriff went out back to shave and wash up, was about through when the turnkey arrived with the day's mail.

One letter from Head Office asking for an explanation on his lack of progress; a complaint from a nester about someone poisoning his well with a dead sheep; a plain letter from Metal City which didn't look very interesting, yet was.

Metal City was just one of many places whose aid Ike had been enlisting as he cast his net wider and wider for a lead on the thieves. His tired eyes opened wider as he scanned the sheriff's lines. Seemed a vacationing deputy who'd been hunting back in the Sierras recently took a short cut via remote Squaw Valley where he had glimpsed from a distance certain suspicious activity involving Reece Hatchette, a dealer known to Metal City law, and a small bunch of cattle wearing the scrolled SR brand of Spanish Ranch, plus two 'hardcases'.

The description of the two men was sketchy; a slim flashy-looking man, the other tall and strongly built. But it was the deputy's eyes for horseflesh that captured Watson's attention. 'The big man rode a red horse and the other was astride a mouse-colored mare, the kind we call a grulla,' he wrote.

Ike stared from the window. He'd seen but one horse of that particular gray in Wolflock and it belonged to Slim Forte, gunfighter and mystery man around town. And belatedly he realized that 'a big man on a red horse' could easily fit Clint – or James Clinton Eastman – another man whose presence and purpose here was now largely a mystery also.

He read and reread the letter several times before identifying it for what it was. A breakthrough! There had been vague suspicions about Slim Forte for months, while it was common knowledge that Clint harbored a huge grudge against Morgan Bowden. Might that grudge be powerful enough to drive Clint to avenge himself against Bowden's ranch any way he could, as this new information suggested?

Suddenly the sheriff of Wolflock wasn't weary any longer. For this information, distasteful as part of it might be, certainly appeared something far stronger than anything he'd been able to get on the rustlers thus far.

He didn't confide in anyone; there was nobody he

could tell. Instead he went searching for anyone who might know when Forte or Clint were to visit town again, as was their habit.

It was late afternoon when, emerging from the Forty-niner Diner, Ike glimpsed Slim Forte riding in from the north.

# CHAPTER 10

# VENGEANCE DAY

Slim Forte propped sharply when he came round the corner to bring the Commission House complex into full view. Instead of the customary late-afternoon flow of workers and clients there was a sizable bunch of men and women gathered before the long front gallery being addressed by . . . Rachel?

'Hell!'

The outlaw was peeved. On the very day he wanted everything quiet and normal here, something unusual was taking place.

But what?

It didn't take long to find out. Rachel Bowden had taken it upon herself to address a gathering of concerned staff and customers regarding the deteriorating crime situation in the region. She was now attempting to convince them that, with the sheriff so plainly overworked, and her uncle at his wits' end over recent heavy stock-losses and troubles at the mine, then surely it was time the Wolflock citizenry recognized their own civic responsibilities. She was suggesting the town banded together to combat the erosion of law and order exemplified by some kind of ongoing riot out at the mine and the rustling from Spanish Ranch.

The girl was convincing and eloquent.

Forte told her so later, after the crowd had dispersed and he sought her out in the clerical section. Rachel was cool. Their friendship had deteriorated since the arrival of Clint upon the scene. Slim Forte was smiling, but was mad as hell. It made him even madder after he raised the matter of Clint's alleged grudge against her uncle, and she actually seemed to side with the tall man from Colorado. It appeared that Bowden had done little but hit the bottle since the allegations of the manner in which he was said to have virtually gypped Henry Eastman out of his partnership in their company, and his niece accepted his heavy drinking as an admission of guilt.

Forte looked around. His main objective in coming here was to ascertain that normal conditions prevailed – before they moved in tonight. He was happy to note that security appeared much lighter than usual; Bowden had been siphoning men away from his house and business installations and putting them to guarding his herds in recent times.

'You seem edgy today, Slim. Anything wrong?'

'Huh?' He scowled. He studied her, aware that he wanted her now more than ever. If only she knew what he was prepared to do to get her, then maybe she would realize that Clint was just a stumblebum by comparison. But he would have her. By the time he was through with both Clint and her uncle, he was going to look like a combination of Kit Carson and a Rockefeller in her eyes.

'Anything wrong?' he echoed, throwing her a farewell salute. 'Just the opposite, honey . . . things never looked better. See you soon, Rache. Still crazy about you, you know?'

Her smile was perfunctory. No warmth. Bitch!

He strode lithely away through the honeycomb of tiny offices with their bulging pigeon-holes of documents, past the dark warehouse aisles smelling of tea and green coffee or rope and saddles, of boots and leather, of bacon and lard, of the oily smell of hardware, the sharp scent of tobacco . . . the omnipresent stink of money.

Bowden's kingdom. And he was about to bring it down. Him – the poor boy from nowhere. He'd already weakened and all but crippled the limbs of the Bowden giant, namely the Font and the ranch. Now it was time to destroy the heart, the Commission House, which he would rebuild when everything here was his.

Despite his emotions, he remained sharp enough to note carefully the position of the night sentries as he strode away across the tracks. Same as usual. He knew them like the back of his hand by this. His men had had the house under observation for weeks.

His men.

At that very moment his full force was heading in from different directions, in ones and twos, gearing up for the big one. And by the time he reached the Prairie Dog, tall Clint was already there, right on schedule, nursing a beer at the gloomy back bar.

Forte stood unseen in an alcove, intently studying the man, his face gleaming like a wet knife-blade. The past months of discipline had been painfully hard for a volatile and violent man of the gun. But tonight he was going to be able at last to let out some rope, let himself go, and enjoy the fulfilling of his plans. The Commission House. Clint. This whole stinking uppity town. All would hurt, and he would do the hurting. And it felt good.

Blanking his features and tugging his hat low over his eyes, he quit the alcove and stepped inside, unaware as he had been ever since his arrival in town that he had picked up a shadow.


The night which Clint was convinced would prove the worst of his life was ushered in by a golden lovers' moon which rose up from behind Frightful Mountain so serenely and peacefully that it seemed to mock him for the way he was feeling.

And what he was feeling was guilt-ridden, uncertain, weak-kneed and sick.

This was no way that any tough man with a mission to fulfill should be shaping up to his moment of truth – that was for sure.

He prowled restlessly along a back street through Old Town, where it was supper-time with strumming guitars, urchins squabbling and the occasional passing of a solitary shadowy horseman.

The horsemen were gun-toting rustlers emerging from hiding to converge upon the railroad tracks. Clint knew what was happening. He alone knew it but there was nothing he could or would do about it, as he was part of it.

He'd known all along it couldn't last. The charmed run he'd had with the gang, that was. Due largely to his comprehensive organization of the major raids which had rocked Spanish Ranch recently, nobody had been killed. He was proud of this fact, for it had enabled him to participate in launching the mortal blows against Bowden without getting blood on his hands.

But Morgan Bowden was far from finished, wouldn't be while the monument to his prosperity stood proud by the railroad tracks. The Commission House complex must go. Forte had determined that it must burn tonight. Clint had his vengeance at his fingertips, yet felt he was coming apart like a sick horse.

There must be killing tonight.

People would die.

Some of them innocent.

Sure, Forte had done his usual meticulous planning in order to have the sentries taken out of the play silently and bloodlessly by his men, leaving the way open for himself and Clint to torch the complex, with everyone to be well and truly gone from the scene by the time the alarm was raised.

Smooth as silk.

Clint knew he couldn't fault the plan, any more than he could honestly believe that anything this big and daring could possibly go off without a hitch. What about the chance passer-by? he'd reflected. Or the night guard out of his correct position for some reason just when the rustlers were moving in to take him out? A dozen things could go wrong and well might, he reasoned. And where would that leave him? Up to his eyes in it, a gun in his fist and no option but to use it.

He stopped on a corner to light a cigarette, the brief flare of the match revealing deep-cut creases in his cheeks and shadows beneath the eyes. He looked up at that moon and forced himself to reflect upon his father and the more than twenty years of his life he'd spent in pain and poverty due to one trusted friend's crookedness and greed.

It worked, succeeding in fanning his anger and banishing the weakening thoughts that might have undermined his iron sense of purpose.

In moments he was whole and hard again. Iron hard.

No dwelling on morality, possible aftermaths, even of the woman he loved. More than ever before, this surely was the time to keep focused on the cause that had driven him to quit Colorado and make this long journey of attrition to the south.

The sacred cause, as he thought of it.

And in its name, he would pay Bowden out. Destroy the bastard as he should be destroyed. And should that entail taking risks and crossing boundaries he would never dream of doing normally, then so be it. This was the hour he'd waited and plotted for over the long years, and not even his conscience would stop him grabbing it with both hands and making it all his own.

He quickened his pace.

He found Slim Forte waiting for him as arranged hard by the switch line where empty freight cars stood in shadowy silence. He didn't expect to find the gunman anything but cocky and supremely confident, and that was exactly how he was. Chewing an unlit cigar and attired in concealing black for the occasion, as was Clint himself, Forte somehow appeared bigger, more formidable and even more dangerous-looking than he'd ever seen him. The man radiated a chilling confidence as he delivered a last-minute review of the battle plan.

'We wait until Hawke and Gilroy take out the two sentries at the south end. Then we cut across with these.' He paused to indicate the oil-soaked torches leaning against a train wheel. 'We fire the south end while the boys are still running down the security northside. Then Titus and Reece put their torches through the windows that end . . . and we're off across to the water tank where the horses are tied, and skedaddle. You got all that in your head, Colorado?'

Strange, Clint mused. There seemed to be an acid edge to the gunman's tone, something almost malevolent in his glittering eye. Although aware all along that his and Forte's partnership was merely a marriage of convenience, underneath which they were still two very different men who could never be friends, only rivals, none the less they had appeared to hit it off well enough while absorbed in the dangerous chore of cutting the ground out from under Bowden. So why this feeling of suppressed hostility emanating from the other man now?

Nerves, he figured.

Slim must be feeling more jittery than he showed.

That had to be it.

Clint realized that, by contrast, he was actually feeling almost calm and resigned now as they stood shoulder to shoulder staring across gleaming tracks and stacks of heavy black ties to glimpse two stealthy figures break away from a corner stack and ghost off towards the south end of Bowden & Company's monumental storehouses and offices.

It had to be done and was best done now.

They were clear of the cars and moving swiftly when Forte almost tripped, cursing as he propped and stared back.

'What?' Clint hissed.

'Thought I seen somethin' move yonder by the wool-shed.'

'Nothing,' Clint reassured. 'C'mon, the boys have put the sentries down and are moving along the back as planned.'

They covered the last sixty feet of open yardspace to gain the flung moonshadow of the main building without further incident, the unconscious figures of the night-watchers sprawled where they had been felled. Clint was breathing heavily and fingering vestas from his pocket when he felt his Colt leave its holster. He whirled and his own gun muzzle rammed painfully into his short ribs.

Slim Forte wasn't smiling any longer.

'Trail's end, you double-dealing son of a bitch!'

'What?' Clint couldn't figure.

'You and Rache,' Forte snarled. 'That's where you made your big mistake, ploughwalker. You came here to do a job, like me, but you took your eye off the ball when you took up with my girl.'

'You're out of your head, man. But look, we can work this out later—'

'It's all worked out, hero ... like clockwork. They're goin' to find you and your torch right here. And who in this man's town don't know by now you hate Bowden's guts and would give an arm to see him finished? So, you'll take the rap when they find you here among the ashes, and that'll mean they won't be lookin' for us nohow. Startin' to understand now, hick? Bowden will still be busted, I'll move in as planned and me and Rache will live happy ever after and she'll never want anyone to mention your stinking Judas Iscariot name again so long as she lives. Now is that smart plannin' or ain't it – loser?'

Clint didn't even give himself time to think before he let fly with a desperation punch. The other expected it.

Forte was chain-lightning fast as he sidestepped the blow then swayed in close to slam his gun barrel against the side of Clint's head. The last thing Clint remembered was his face smashing into the ballast stones.

There was no telling how long he was out to it. But eventually he began to grow conscious of two things; intense heat and light surrounding him . . . a hand shaking him roughly by the shoulder.

'Clint . . . Eastman, whatever your name is. Get up before you catch fire, man!'

Instinctively, desperately, Clint rolled away from the wall of flame bearing down upon him and came up groggily onto one knee. Blood streamed down his face from his gashed head as he found himself staring foolishly into the grim weather-lined features of Ike Watson.

'Sheriff . . . how. . . ?'

'I've been dogging you both and you're both going to swing for this,' Watson panted, hauling him roughly erect by his shirt collar. 'But I couldn't let you burn even if you might have it coming.'

Clint's head still buzzed like a chainsaw. Yet his mind was coming clearer and increasingly comprehending moment by moment. Forte had belted him unconscious, then left him to be devoured by the inferno – dead and seemingly guilty of arson. And but for the intervention of the dour badgepacker, that would surely have been his fate.

The lawman began to speak again but his words were swallowed by the deep-throated bellow of a revolver. Clint heard the slug strike something with a thud. But it wasn't him. Then he realized that the sheriff was staggering backwards and clutching at his ribs, his face ashen in the hell-ish light of the flames. Instantly Clint slung an arm around the man's back to support him and plucked the second .45 from his shell-belt as Slim Forte's sixshooter bellowed again from fifty yards distant.

Whirling, still supporting the lawman, Clint identified the flame-limned silhouette of the gunman. He stood crouched some distance beyond the southern end of the main building which had long been the town's symbol of power and success, the Commission House, but which by this was totally engulfed by high-leaping pillars of flame.

'You never could keep your long snout out of where it didn't belong, Watson you broken-winded loser!' Forte shouted as he ducked for cover in back of a waist-high stone wall. 'Well, it's gonna cost you, badgeman. You're both maggot-meat – and everyone's gonna believe you heroes shot it out . . . if there's enough left of you to figure out anything, that is!'

His gun belched red and yellow heat and a bullet with his name on it came looking for Clint. But he was no longer where he'd been a split-second before. Instead he moved lightning-fast to seize the wounded lawman and hurl him violently to ground, then he flung himself across Watson's body protectively.

Jerking up his gun, he triggered blindly in the general direction of the half-wall, fully expecting the bullet with his name on it to claim him as he saw the crouching killer's Colt glimmering in the light.

He saw his bullet ricochet off the bricks a split second before a lancing sheet of flaming roofing material sheered away from the conflagration to crash to ground with a muffled roar a bare twenty feet from Forte's position!

'Act o' God!' Watson croaked disbelievingly as both men glimpsed the figure of the cursing gunman roll violently away from his cover and leap to his feet, barely eluding the billowing flames reaching out from the wreckage.

'Get him while he's busy, Clint!'

Clint didn't need any second bidding. His weapon whipped up, he squeezed trigger, the fast-moving figure of Slim Forte spun and hit ground.

The man was hit, but not hard enough.

Swiftly up on one knee, Forte was beckoning others out of their sight to support him as fast-moving Clint heaved a sagging Watson across one shoulder and began to retreat. The indistinct figures of gun-toting rustlers moved into sight through choking smoke and rippling heat haze. They wanted to take flight but Forte overrode them: 'That's the goddamn law!' he screamed. 'We gotta finish those bastards – no witnesses!'

Instantly gunfire lanced through roiling smoke, and a bullet clipped Clint's right leg. Steeling himself against the pain while still placing his body between the sheriff and the enemy, he found himself fanning gun hammer and triggering faster than he would have believed possible, the proximity of violent death pumping his system with adrenaline. He saw a rustler nosedive into flames, screaming hideously as he became a human torch. Forte was angling away from the fiery tongues now, limping and bleeding but still firing fast and fanning gun hammer – a shooting fool.

Clint returned Forte's fire with a crashing volley, pausing only when Watson urgently tugged his shirtsleeve. The lawman was leaking crimson but his voice was clear and strong.

'Can't move on this leg . . . so you hightail it for cover while you still can. I'm done for here and someone's got to be left to name the guilty . . . Run!'

'Don't turn hero on me, lawman,' Clint mouthed, ducking low as death droned close. 'In any case, I'm the freaking guilty party here, so just shut up and—'

The bullet clipped the deltoid muscle of his shoulder, spinning him about and dumping him across the sheriff's body. For desperate moments his vision was distorted, but then it came clear and suddenly Clint found he could see in a way he'd never done before. It was as though he had been forever walking a dark mightmare of his own follish making, but was now suddenly awakened. What a fool he'd been to believe he could be like . . . like Slim Forte!

Thank God he couldn't!

But he could still fight for what was right – could and did.

The sheriff roared angrily at him as he sprang to his feet, reloading from his belt. Ignoring the man, weaving as he moved forward despite his wounds, he was fanning his gun hammer like a professional, knowing he was going to die but desperate now to salvage what little he might of his honor, that Eastman honor his father had maintained all his unhappy life.

Slim Forte suddenly jack-knifed and screamed, a bullet piercing his body. As he fell, another man turned and ran until Clint drilled a slug through his back. It emerged from his chest in a hideous spray of hot crimson. That bleeding, smoking apparition coming up off the ground to take a wild shot at him was Forte. Clint's gun answered with fierce authority and Slim Forte fell dead on his face.

Sixguns roared like savage dogs until a thunderclap

exploded in Clint's skull and the blazing world turned black.

It didn't figure. If he was dead, then howcome it seemed he could still hear Ike Watson's droning voice?

Clint blinked awake and pain gripped him hard – head, shoulder, thigh. He had pain to spare. Yet his senses seemed remarkably clear as he slowly realized that he was in a hospital ward, swathed in linen bandages and feeling, if one could overlook the pain, pretty damn much alive.

'Knew you were only drowsing.' The sheriff sat at his side with one leg bandaged hip to ankle, a set of crutches leaning against his chair. 'Folks are waiting to see you outside but I had to get in first to get a few things clear.'

Clint nodded soberly. Sure. Clear up a few things. Like admit his guilt and let them tell him what he was in for. He'd been a fool, he realized, yet he knew he was never more clear-headed than right at that moment. Not that it would do him any good, he figured; he only wished it might be different.

Forte and four rustlers were dead, the sheriff monotoned, the survivors escaping into the hills. The Commission House had burned to the ground and Bowden had taken to his bed with a bottle while his sons and niece moved in to take over and salvage what was left of the company.

'Get on with it,' Clint interrupted. He was staring out at a patch of precious sky. He had never seen anything more beautiful than that small patch of blue, and wondered just how many high-sky mornings he might get to see before they put a rope around his neck.

'All right,' grunted Watson, getting up onto his crutches. 'Just tell me one thing, mister. If you found yourself in the clear now, what would you do?'

'That's a dumb question.'

'Try and give me a smart answer.'

Clint looked away. 'Well, I guess I'd work just as hard again as I did to get square with Bowden – at . . . at tryin' to make up for what I've done. . . .'

'Thought you'd say that. Well, someone special is waiting to see you, but first there's someone else who's brought you something. . . .'

He stepped back and an apparition took his place. At least that's what the ratty attorney looked like through pain-glazed eyes. But he got to see the man clearly enough as he brandished the satchel of documents Clint had furnished him with, and began talking like a chattering magpie.

Turned out Clackett had travelled all the long way to Sante Fe to consult a former Supreme Court judge of his acquaintance, who proved willing and able to clarify every detail of the original Eastman-Bowden commission business in Colorado and had eventually come up with his summation. Which was: Morgan Bowden was plainly guilty of deceit, fraud, forgery and gross malpractice in the series of 'business' decisions he'd made years earlier resulting in Henry James Eastman losing his half of their mutual successful enterprise.

Clint was dazed as he listened to a triumphant Clackett prattle on about charges, contacting the county sheriff and his judge, planning a date for Bowden to stand up in a court of law and face his accusers – at long last.

In that moment, as Watson ushered the still-talking attorney out, Clint could feel his father in the room . . . until his place was taken by the sheriff again. Ike Watson had company.

'Miss Rachel has been waitin' to see you all night, mister.' The lawman smiled. 'Then later you and me can talk about how best to get this town back on its feet.'

Clint stared. Watson just grinned understandingly.

'Nobody's making any charges against you while I'm sheriff, son. Hell, I knew from the jump you were no crummy avenger. I know why you did what you did. But nobody else knows it all here. Sure, I guess I could charge you and maybe even get to see you locked up a spell. But that would be about as wrong as what Bowden did to your father way back, as I see it. But on your bull-headed way to square accounts, you risked your life to save mine and you killed Slim Forte, saving New Mexico a lot of grief. So I reckon the good you done far outweighs the bad. In any case, we got a whole heap to do here and I've been beggin' for a decent deputy for way too long and . . . hey, no admittance in here, young woman!'

'Close the door on your way out, Sheriff,' she ordered, then gave the man a little nudge to help him on his way. The door clicked shut on the lawman's confused face and she stood at the end of the bed, looking a million dollars but also different somehow.

He soon discovered just how different.

She had hocked his sixshooter, she informed him coolly, stripping off her gloves as she came round the side of his bed. He wouldn't need it any longer, as rebuilding the company would not require any shooting – simply a whole lot of hard work and dedication. As for his injuries, the medico insisted he'd be walking in three days, by which time the town volunteers expected to have the old company site cleared ready to begin construction.

His first post would be as an overseer, and further

promotion up the ladder would depend entirely upon his attitude.

'What the hell—?' he began, but this new authoritative woman cut him off.

'You might well be the town hero today, and perhaps Sheriff Watson is right in insisting you have no charges to answer. But don't think that doesn't mean you don't have changes to make.'

'What sort of changes?'

'I'll show you,' she replied calmly, 'even though I'm not sure I should.' He was protesting as she sat on the bed edge and leaned close. But he fell silent and disbelieving and was no longer objecting to her take-charge attitude as her lips came softly against his and seemed to hold there for an eternity – or at least long enough for one driven loner to understand fully that she was promising something that he had never experienced before.

Something called love.

He reached for her again but she rose smartly, blushing only slightly.

'You really didn't deserve all that,' she teased smilingly. 'But then, you are a hero, after all.'

The man who'd come to Wolflock, New Mexico, searching for revenge would be first to admit he didn't feel like any hero, certainly didn't feel he deserved any of this. Nevertheless, Clint knew he would still be reaching out to claim it all with both arms. With all his heart.